PUCKING FORBIDDEN HEARTS

PUCKING DARK HEARTS
BOOK 2

MAGGIE ALABASTER

Cover design by Carol Marques

Edited by Lily Luchesi

Proofread by Nora Hogan

TRIGGER WARNINGS

This story contains some sensitive topics:

Forced pregnancy

Violence

Threats of sexual assault

Consensual non-consent

CHAPTER 1

MARLEY

I locked the door behind the last patient of the day and leaned my back against it, my eyes closed for a moment.

"It was a long day."

My eyes snapped open and I startled, bumping my hip on the door handle.

Doctor Oliver Ryan looked at me with a combination of amusement and concern. "Didn't mean to scare you."

"You didn't, I just—" I pushed my glasses back up my nose and cleared my throat. "I didn't see you there." I stepped past him, back to my desk.

I switched off the computer and turned around to find him standing right behind me.

I let out a soft breath of surprise, but didn't move. I couldn't. We stood almost chest to chest, my ass pressed against the edge of the desk. Heat radiated off his body like a wave of lava, threatening to pour down over me.

"If I didn't know better, I'd think you were avoiding me." He spoke in a low, rumbly tone that got me going from head to toe.

"Of course I'm not," I protested. "How could I? This practice isn't *that* big." It was nothing more than a reception desk and three treatment rooms. The other general practitioners only worked a couple of days a week, leaving us alone more often than not.

"That's true. There's nowhere to hide here." He leaned in, until his lips were no more than a centimetre or two away from mine.

"I don't want to hide, but we need to—"

A loud tapping on the door made me jump for the second time in a handful of minutes. We sprang apart so fast, I bumped my ass on the back of the desk.

"I'll see who that is." With a regretful sigh, Oliver walked over to unlock and open the door. "Cat! You're looking radiant."

"Hey, Dad." Catalina Ryan stepped into the surgery and kissed her father on the cheek. "Did you forget we have a date for dinner?"

She walked past him to give me an awkward hug, her pregnant belly getting between us somewhat. "Is my father keeping you here too late again?" She turned her teasing smile on Oliver.

"Um, no." If she'd arrived a few minutes later, she

might have found me bent over the desk, her beloved father pounding into me. The thought made my face hot. We had to be more careful.

"I was just leaving." I stepped around to the other side of my desk and grabbed my bag and phone.

"You should join us," Cat said. "I don't see enough of you or Eden."

"We had dinner together…" I had to stop and think. "Yeah, it has been a while." The three of us were close friends, but the last year had been hectic. Cat was often busy with her three boyfriends, Shaw, Easton and Cruz. Now with a baby on the way, she'd be busier than ever.

"Then you should come," Cat said. "Right, Dad? You don't mind, do you?"

Oliver arched an eyebrow slightly. "Yes, Marley should *come*." He put the slightest emphasis on the last word, subtle enough for his daughter to miss, but making my face heat further. "I don't mind at all."

"Great." Cat hooked her arm through mine and pulled me towards the door. "It's not often I get a night away from the guys with two of my favourite people."

I glanced over my shoulder to Oliver, but he smiled and grabbed up his phone and bag, and locked the door behind us.

"The guys must be excited," I said. "The season is about to start and they get to use their own, brand-new stadium."

The Opal Springs Ghouls were one of the newest

teams to join the AIHL, something they'd worked toward for a long time. If anyone in town wasn't a fan of ice hockey before, they were converted by now. The construction of the arena generated so many jobs and was a huge boost to the whole town.

"I don't think the arena is big enough," Cat said dryly. "The whole team has been treated like rock stars for the last few months. Their heads are getting enormous."

In spite of her words, she smiled, if a little wryly. All three of her boyfriends were on the team and she loved them, egos and all. Even after they hell they'd put her through when they first met.

"Just when I thought they couldn't get bigger egos," I said with a smile.

We walked across the road to one of the newer restaurants in town, Sticks. They served everything from steak to grilled fish. All fancier than we were used to in Opal Springs. The boom brought in a bunch of new businesses. This was one of my favourites.

The other being a place that sold adult toys. A girl could never have too many vibrators.

"Nothing you can't handle." Oliver didn't attempt to hide his scrutiny of Cat's leg.

Badly broken last year, she sometimes struggled with it, especially when she didn't rest when she should. If she was good at anything, it was pushing herself too hard. As her father and her doctor, he was always watching out for her.

She gave him a look, clearly neither missing what he was doing, nor impressed with it. "Stop fussing," she told him.

He raised his hands to either side. "I didn't say a thing."

"But you were thinking it." She slipped into a seat at the round table, leaving Oliver and I to sit beside each other.

"Would you prefer I stop giving a shit?" he asked.

"No, but I'm a grown woman. I can take care of myself." She picked up her menu and started to read.

"Yes, you can. We're all adults here." Oliver squeezed my knee under the table. "Capable of making our own choices."

I thought for a moment he was going to tell her about us, but instead he picked up his menu and scanned it.

My heart racing, I did the same.

"It's so nice of you to join Dad and I," Cat said to me. "I keep telling him he should get out more, but you know what he's like. It's time he met someone, don't you think?"

"Um, sure." I adjusted my glasses and cleared my throat. Oliver's hand on my knee was distracting. I was sure Cat must be able to see right through us.

On the other hand, I wished she would. We'd been sneaking around behind her back for long enough.

"Maybe I have met someone and I haven't told you," Oliver said. His fingers tightened around my thigh before sneaking up slowly and slipping between my legs. "I'm also an adult, believe it or not." His thumb stroked over the front of my pants, brushing past my clit.

"If you've met someone, I'm happy for you," Cat said easily. "When do we get to meet her? Or him. We won't judge, will we, Marley? We want you to be happy."

"Of course we do." My voice was higher as he swiped his thumb back across the front of my pants. "Have you decided what you're having for dinner?"

"No, but I know what I want for dessert," Oliver said. He smiled at me as if he was completely innocent, and looked back at his menu.

"Typical Dad, always wanting to go straight to dessert," Cat teased. "He's always had a sweet tooth."

"Always," Oliver agreed. He pressed his thumb against my clit and rubbed it firmly.

I swallowed. If he kept doing that, I was going to come right here, in front of his daughter. "I think I'll have the vegetarian lasagne."

"Not in the mood for meat tonight?" Oliver asked.

Before I could respond, Cat grimaced and pushed herself to her feet. "Sorry, I need to pee. This baby is sitting right on my bladder. I'll be right back."

"Take your time," Oliver said.

I waited until she was safely away to look at him square on, my eyes wide. "We can't keep lying to her." I grabbed his wrist and pulled his hand away from my pussy. "Or doing things like this. Someone might see. *She* might see."

He rested his forearm against the edge of the table. "Do you want to end it?"

"No," I said quickly. I closed my eyes and sighed out my nose. "Unless you won't tell her. I'm not sneaking around behind her back anymore. I want to be with you, but she's my best friend. If she knew we were lying to her, she'd be angry at both of us. After everything she's been through, she deserves to be happy. She needs to know she can trust the people around her."

"Then we tell her," he said. "We pick the right time and place and sit her down to explain everything."

"Do you think she'll understand?" I said. "She's made it clear she doesn't like the idea you and I could even be *attracted* to each other, much less...anything else. I don't want to come between you and her. I also don't want to put her under stress while she's pregnant."

"Is everything okay?" Cat slipped back into her chair. "You two look intense."

"We were discussing a new patient," Oliver said. "We're both concerned her physical health might be negatively impacted by her mental health."

That wasn't wrong. Including the part about her being his patient. She had her own OB/GYN, but her father was involved with her care as much as he could be. And we *were* talking about her mental health. Specifically, the result of her potential anger when she found out we were fucking.

"Oh. If anyone can help her, it will be both of you," Cat said. She rested her hands on her belly.

"I haven't asked how you're feeling," I said. "You look amazing. Pregnancy agrees with you. Are the guys looking after you?"

She snorted softly. "I'm surprised they let me out tonight. They've been fussing over me like three mother hens. Or father cocks." She exchanged a glance and a smile with Oliver.

A private joke, I presumed.

"They're all going to take care of the baby?" I asked.

"Absolutely," she agreed. "They're going to make amazing fathers. They don't even care if we never do a paternity test. As far as they're concerned, they're all the father."

She may never know which of her three boyfriends was the biological father of her baby. It didn't surprise me that none of them cared. That was just biology. What happened after the baby was born was what mattered.

"That's wonderful." I couldn't contain a slight jab of envy. Cat was the ambitious one, almost making the Winter Olympic team at speed skating, and now she was qualified veterinarian. That pregnant glow made the gorgeous redhead even more beautiful.

I'd always seen myself settling down and focusing on a family, not a career. If I was pregnant, I'd probably look like a blonde sausage trying to escape its skin. I couldn't help yearning anyway.

"It's wonderful," Oliver agreed.

He reminded me if I was pregnant, it would be with Cat's sibling. The baby growing in her belly was his grandchild. He was still only forty-eight, but it felt as though the situation got more complicated the bigger her bump got.

I glanced over to see him give me a long look. I couldn't tell what he was thinking. I didn't think he was planning on telling her about us tonight, but what else was going through his head, I didn't know. He was complicated at best. An excellent doctor and a wonderful father. Not to mention an incredible lover. No one ever made me feel the way he did, physically or emotionally.

I knew he cared about me. I cared about him too. This whole thing would be a lot easier if we didn't both also care about Cat. Neither of us wanted to hurt her, or get hurt ourselves.

"You're both coming to the game on Saturday night, aren't you?" Cat asked. "The Ghouls are playing the Dusk Bay Demons in the first round. We need all the help we can get to cheer the team on."

"I wouldn't miss it," Oliver said.

"Eden and I will be there," I said. "It's not every day you get to sit in the team's box and watch them kick Demons' asses." I didn't say so, but I wasn't sure if that would happen.

The Demons won the cup last season. They'd be hard to beat, but the Ghouls were hungry. They'd give it a red hot go.

"I'll introduce you to the new goalie," Cat said to me. "I think you'll like him."

I resisted the urge to glance at Oliver and simply smiled. "I look forward to it." Why did I feel as though I'd just tangled myself deeper in a spiderweb?

CHAPTER 2
MARLEY

Oliver and I walked Cat to her car. Under the guise of being a gentleman, he helped her inside. She tried not to let on, but we both saw the discomfort in her leg before she settled into the seat.

He watched her drive away with a furrowed brow.

"She'll be okay," I said.

"Only if she follows the doctor's advice." He slipped his arm around my waist and we crossed the road back to our own cars, parked side by side in a now darkened parking lot.

"Does she ever?" I asked. "They say doctors are the worst patients, but their relatives must come a close second."

He chuckled. "When those children are athletes, they are definitely the worst. Much worse than doctors." He glanced over at me and arched his eyebrows.

"I call bullshit on that." I unlocked my car and tossed

my bag and phone onto the seat. Before I could turn around, he grabbed me from behind, his firm hands flat against my belly.

"Is that so?" He nuzzled into my neck, his erection poking into my hip.

"Absolutely," I said unapologetically. "What are you going to do about it?"

"For disrespecting your boss, and potentially the whole medical profession, you can choke on my cock." He turned me around and pushed me down onto my knees. "Take him out."

Eagerly, I slid down Oliver's zipper and pushed his trousers and black boxers down to free his erection. He was thick and hard, pre-cum already glistening on his tip.

I licked my lips.

Oliver grabbed my ponytail and brought my face closer before tapping the head of his cock against my lips. "Open up."

"What if I don't?" I asked.

He looked down at me and cocked his head. "Then I have a wooden spoon with your name on it."

I shivered and grinned before I opened my mouth and slipped my lips around his tip. I swirled my tongue around his head, tasting his saltiness, teasing him until he groaned.

He tightened his grip on my hair and pushed himself deeper into my mouth. All the way in until I gagged.

"That's better." He held himself there for a few moments before starting to thrust, fucking my mouth deep and hard. "You know what to do if it gets too much."

I did. All I had to do was tap his leg three times and he'd stop. I'd only had to tap out once, when I was stuffy from hayfever. Fucking Spring.

Aside from that, I loved blowing him. I loved the way he felt and tasted, the way he groaned as he used my mouth.

This was how it started between us. With me on my knees, his cock filling my mouth. I couldn't remember how it happened now, but we hadn't been able to keep our hands off each other since. Unless Cat was around.

When I thought he was about to come, he slipped out of my mouth and pulled me to my feet. He opened the back door of my car and pressed me inside. Grabbing the front of my pants, he undid them and slid them and my panties down all the way to my ankles.

He knelt beside the car, pulled me to the edge of the seat and opened my legs. Eyes on my face he slid a finger inside my pussy, then another.

"Fucking hell, Marley-Jane, you're so wet." He slid in another finger and thumb.

Slowly, he fucked me with his hand before pulling my pants off one foot so he could spread my legs wider. He grabbed my hips, wrapped my legs around his waist and slid me onto his cock.

I lay back on the seat and worked my hand under my mohair jumper to rub my fingers over my nipples.

"That's my girl," he crooned. "You feel so fucking good. I'll never get enough of being inside you." He closed his eyes and savoured the connection between our bodies.

I couldn't get enough of this either. Everything in the world evaporated, leaving only us and this moment.

I pressed my heels into his ass, encouraging him to push himself deeper.

He grabbed my legs, draped them over his shoulders and started to thrust into me with firm, even strokes. He was so deep inside me, I felt him all the way through, everywhere.

So fucking full.

"God, Oliver," I said breathlessly. "Yes, fuck me harder."

"Anything for you, my beautiful girl." He pounded, driving me into the seat with each thrust. He gripped my hips with bruising fingers, holding me in place.

"I'm going to come." I pinched my nipples through the lace of my bra, arched my back and rocked myself against him. "Come with me. Come inside me."

One of the benefits of sleeping with a doctor, we knew we were both clean. He kept my birth control up-to-date, so we could fuck bareback the way we both wanted to. He liked nothing better than to fill my pussy with his cum.

He groaned and ground into me, pulling an orgasm out of both of us at the same time.

Fireworks exploded around us. I was dragged down in a whirlpool of bliss before gradually trickling out the other side.

I flopped back against the seat, trying to catch my breath as he did the same.

Finally, he slid out of me and lowered my legs. He did up his pants and reached into his bag for a packet of wet wipes. Like he always did, he carefully cleaned me up, wiping his cum from my pussy.

"Go and pee," he told me. "I'll wait here for you."

Another benefit of screwing a doctor, he always made sure I was looked after when we fucked. He wanted me clean and without a UTI.

"I won't be long." I pulled my pants and panties back on and grabbed the keys to unlock the surgery so I could use the toilet.

I locked the door behind me and quickly trotted back to our cars. I didn't have to hurry, I knew he wouldn't leave while I was here. He'd never leave a woman alone in the dark, especially after what happened to Cat.

I tossed my keys back into the car and straightened up to let him wind his arms around me.

"This is wrong," he said softly.

My heart sank. "You regret fucking me in the back of my car?" That stung more than it should.

We never talked about a future for us. Maybe he didn't see one. This might just have been a fling between us and his office manager. Never intended to last more than a little while. Maybe lying to his daughter was getting to him.

He leaned back and frowned at me. "I've never regretted fucking you, Marley-Jane. Never. What's wrong is that you're going home to your place and I'm going home to mine. To one cat and a goldfish."

Cat had moved in with her boyfriends months ago. "I want you with me when I fall asleep at night. When I wake up in the morning. Saying goodbye to you every day is wrong. Hard. Difficult. "

"If we tell her," I said tentatively. "And she doesn't freak out. Once the town gossip dies down we can."

Opal Springs was small enough that they'd talk about what a doctor was doing regardless of what it was, but especially if it was *me* he was doing.

"That sounds like a lot of ifs and whens." He sighed.

"It is, but nothing we can't deal with." I stood on my toes and pressed my mouth to his. He tasted lightly of red wine and some kind of spice. He always tasted so good, I wanted more and more. I wanted to drag him back into my car and wrap my legs around him again.

The car beside mine beeped and flashed as someone unlocked it. That was quickly followed by footsteps walking past and stopping to glance at us. We sprang apart, but not before they saw us with our tongues virtually down each other's throats.

"Sorry." He was about six foot four, and around the same age as me. In the light coming from the surgery, I made out brown hair, black jeans and a faded black Henley. "I didn't mean to interrupt." He spoke in an American drawl.

"We were just leaving anyway," Oliver said quickly. He opened the driver's side door of my car and gave me a meaningful look.

"Right, it's getting late." I smiled at them both before ducking quickly into my car.

Oliver closed the door behind me and stepped back. I grabbed up my keys and started the engine.

We were lucky the guy hadn't happened past ten minutes earlier, he would have caught us mid-fuck. Although, he was clearly not from Opal Springs. Chances were I'd never see him again.

I gave Oliver a small wave and backed my car out of my space. The other guy stood a few metres away, watching while I drove out to the road and headed away.

Before they were out of sight, I glanced over my shoulder to see them both getting into their own cars.

Oliver was right. Having to say goodbye at the end of the evening sucked. We'd have to find a way to be together before the situation drove us apart forever. I just hoped like hell Cat wouldn't hate me. I didn't want to lose either of them and I sure as fuck didn't want to have to choose between them. That would be an impossible decision. One that would rip out my heart and break it into a million tiny pieces.

No, there had to be a way to make everyone happy. One way or another.

CHAPTER 3
MARLEY

"This is incredible." I was staring, but I couldn't bring myself to care.

The team box in Opal Springs Arena was a world away from the stands we used to have. Plush chairs and new tables were dotted around the room, most facing the window that looked down over the ice. Along one wall was a table covered in plates of food. Behind that, the wall was decorated with the team logo. In the centre of the room, the logo adorned the floor.

The box was full of family and friends of the Ghouls, talking and laughing in small groups.

I recognised Saxon Davies, twin brother of Cole, the team's right defence.

Saxon was a prop for the Opal Springs Fury, the rugby union team. Right now, he was basking in the attention of three women. He and his twin were good-looking as hell. Saxon, in particular, knew it. Whenever I saw him, he had women hanging off him, and arrogance to spare.

Cole was the quieter of the two. I couldn't remember having seen him with anyone, now I thought about it. I'd always had a bit of a crush on him, but from a safe distance.

No doubt he was as in demand as his brother, he was just more subtle about it.

"It really is amazing," Cat agreed.

She'd had a tour of the facilities a few weeks ago with her guys, so none of this was new to her. She still seemed as impressed as Eden and me.

"It's good to have the guys here. I can skate at the community rink without them interrupting me." She grimaced, but she'd eventually forgiven them for the trouble they gave her when she was trying to practice her speed skating.

"No," Oliver told her.

She rolled her eyes at him and settled into a chair near the window. "I wasn't planning to try for a comeback."

He rolled his eyes back at her. "You forget all three of us know you better than that. If you thought you could, you'd go for it."

"He's right, you know." I sat beside Cat, where I could keep half an eye on the ice and the other half on Oliver. I wanted to sit beside him, but that might raise Eden and Cat's eyebrows.

"Did you pay her to say that?" Cat teased.

"No, I'm just always right," Oliver said smugly. "I don't need to pay Marley anything extra to agree. Right, Marley?"

I pretended to contemplate for a moment. "I'm always open to the idea of a pay raise. Maybe I should insist on one in return for stroking your ego."

Judging by the way his eyes darkened, it wasn't his ego he was thinking of me stroking. Of course, now I was doing the same thing, picturing my hand curled around his cock.

"I don't think I've met a man who needed his ego stroked," Eden remarked. "Do they exist outside Opal Springs?"

"Not in Melbourne," Cat said. "Not that I met anyway. It might be a universal thing."

Oliver huffed. "Us men are as sensitive as women are. We all need to be told we're amazing from time to time."

"Dad, you're amazing." Cat leaned over to give him a hug.

"Thanks, but as my daughter, you're obligated to say that." He returned her hug and patted her back lightly. His words were accompanied with a loving smile that made my heart melt. They were as close as father and daughter could be.

I'd seen him with young patients a million times. He loved most people, but children in particular. There was something incredibly sexy about a guy who liked kids.

Every time I saw him with them, my ovaries sat up and took notice. Did he want more children, or was Cat and her little sister, Bree, enough?

"Marley and Eden think you're amazing too," she assured him. "You're like a second father to both of them, right girls?"

"Absolutely," Eden agreed.

I swallowed. Oliver was more like a daddy than a father, but all I could do was nod and squeak out, "Sure. Look, the guys are warming up."

That was the perfect way to change the subject. All eyes were immediately on the ice, where the Ghouls and the Demons were stepping out onto the rink.

My gaze followed Phoenix DiMarco, the Demons' goalie, as he knelt down to do groin stretches.

"I'll never not want to watch goalies warm up," I said.

"I can do that," Oliver remarked.

"Dad!" Cat slapped him lightly on the chest. "None of us needs to think about you doing those."

I hoped like hell my face wasn't bright red right then. My head was about to combust from the mental image of Oliver lying over me, his body moving back and forth as he thrust into me.

Oliver chuckled. I wasn't sure if it was directed at his daughter or me. Maybe both. He was enjoying stirring us both up. He was such a brat at times. It was one of the things I liked most about him, but if he wasn't careful, Cat was going to catch on. Or Eden would.

I gave him a warning look, which he responded to with a wink. Fortunately, Cat's attention was on the ice, watching her three guys. Easton and Cruz seemed to be teasing each other, judging by the grins on both of their faces. Shaw shook his head at them both and skated down to the other side of the rink.

"They must be excited," I said. If I was them, I'd be so nervous I'd want to pee myself.

"They are," she agreed. "Easton was saying the other day they feel like all their dreams came true." She rested her hands on her belly.

"Those boys are lucky you forgave them," Oliver said darkly. "For a while there, I was ready to throttle them with my bare hands." He made a strangling gesture with his hands, moving them back and forth like he was choking the living shit out of someone.

The protective side of such a caring man was hot as hell. Would he throttle someone if they did something to me?

"Lucky for all of us there's no need for that," Cat said. "And Dean Hayes is dead, so I'm free to get on with my life."

Dean was the Ghouls' former goalie. He died of a nasty case of the flu, according to Oliver. Nothing he didn't deserve, I guessed. It sounded like a particularly horrible way to go.

Her eyes glazed whenever she mentioned him, which wasn't often. What he did to her that night would live with her forever. I knew she still occasionally had nightmares about it. No one would blame her for that. If it was me, I'd come apart at the seams. Cat was one of the strongest people I'd ever met.

"I'm happy for you," I said sincerely.

"I know you're going to meet someone amazing," Cat said. "Both of you deserve to have your own happily ever after. You too, Dad."

"And if I don't, I have Lucifer, the cat, to keep me company," Oliver said.

Cat leaned over to pat him on the arm. "Poor Dad. Maybe you should cut back your hours a bit and get out more. It can't be healthy to work all those hours. Right, Marley?"

"Right," I said. He didn't work quite as many hours as she might think he did. Of course, I wasn't going to tell her what he did with those other hours, as tempted as I was. She really should know what he and I were up to. Okay, not the specifics, but that we had a relationship that went beyond boss and employee.

"I'm here now, aren't I?" Oliver asked.

"Yes, you are, and I'm going to insist you come to the pub with us after the game," Cat said. "You never know who you might meet."

Oliver shrugged. "Who am I to argue with a pregnant woman?"

"Exactly." Cat nodded. "Marley, Eden and I will keep an eye out for the perfect woman for you."

"Maybe I've already met her." Oliver didn't meet my

gaze. Instead he looked at his daughter, an eyebrow raised.

Cat narrowed her eyes at him. "You have? Are you seeing someone and you didn't tell me?"

"I might be," Oliver said, looking cagey. "I don't have to tell you everything. Last time I looked, I was the parent around here."

"We want to meet her," Cat said immediately. She looked like she might bounce out of her seat. "Right, girls?" She looked around at Eden and me.

"Absolutely," Eden agreed.

I cleared my throat. "Yeah, sure. Definitely." Or maybe a hole could open up under my chair and swallow me up instead.

"Why don't you send her a message and invite her to the pub?" Cat suggested. "What's one more person? Unless she doesn't like crowds."

"She loves crowds," Oliver said.

"The game is starting," I said, gesturing towards the ice. With any luck, that would end the conversation for now. Before things got even more awkward. If that was possible.

All eyes turned down to the game. The excitement level rose, laced with a dose of anxiety. The first game of the season was an important one and the guys had a lot to prove.

The worst thing that could happen would be for them to fall on their faces after everything they'd done to get here. All the work they'd put in. Like any professional sporting team, they were all replaceable if they didn't perform.

In front of their home crowd, in a brand-new arena, they'd want to win, and they'd want it badly.

"I can't breathe," Eden said with a laugh.

"Neither can I," Cat agreed.

"Remember when we had to convince you to come to a game with us?" I teased. "You were absolutely certain you'd hate every minute of it. Now, here you are, practically a puck bunny."

"I remember," she said. "That feels like a hundred lifetimes ago."

I turned my attention back to the ice as the puck was dropped and both teams snapped into action.

The Demons centre took possession of the puck and skated into the Ghouls' defensive zone, pushing it out in front of him like he had all day.

It was Shaw who intercepted him and stole the puck before sliding it over to Cole Davies.

The crowd cheered, but it was short-lived. The Demons took back possession a few moments later and scored the first goal of the game.

In the box, we collectively groaned, but the guys skated back into position, their focus firmly intact.

For the next ten minutes, we sat on the edges of our seats. The guys switched in and out every thirty seconds, their coach, Kage Foster, gesturing at them and keeping them on track.

Moments before the end of the first period, the Ghouls' new goalie stopped the puck a hair from the goal, stopping the Demons from scoring again. The Demons' centre, Coast Riggs, had snapped the puck towards the goal at an impossible angle, making the save all the more impressive.

Even those in the audience who were cheering for the Demons cheered for the goalie this time. His face hidden behind his mask, I couldn't see his expression, but he nodded his acknowledgement of their appreciation.

The period ended before the guys could resume their places. Instead, they stepped off the ice to have a break and a drink of water.

"That was so exciting," Eden said. "I don't think I've seen a game that exciting before."

"They're playing in the big leagues now," I said.

Granted, the AIHL wasn't the big leagues compared to North American hockey, but this was a step up from playing as amateurs. Someday maybe, they'd be raking in millions.

"They are, but they have what it takes to win," Cat said. "There's no reason they can't beat the Demons."

"Of course there isn't," I said.

I pushed my glasses back in place and turned my attention back to the ice as the second period started. My attention kept going back to the goalie. After that save, I was intrigued to know about the guy behind the mask. Cat said she'd introduce us.

I'd make sure she did, if only to satisfy my curiosity.

Although, maybe Oliver would tell her what was going on if he thought I was interested in someone else. I didn't like playing games, but sooner or later we'd have to come clean. If I gave that a little nudge, then where was the harm?

CHAPTER 4
MARLEY

The mood at O'Reilly's pub was sombre. The Ghouls put up a good fight, but they were beaten five goals to one. As they say, the Demons were the better team on the day.

"We'll kick their asses next time." Easton draped an arm over Cat's shoulders.

"Of course you will," I said. "That was just a warmup."

He grinned at me and offered me a fist bump. I bumped before grabbing Eden's hand and pulling her towards the bar.

"Time to have some fun." I ordered a vodka and orange juice and tapped my phone on the card reader.

Eden ordered hers and leaned sideways against the bar. "You didn't have fun watching the game?"

"Of course I did, but this is even more fun." The bar

attendant placed my drink in front of me. I nodded my thanks and slipped a straw in before taking a sip.

"So good." I toasted Eden and tried not to look at Oliver, who stood amongst the crowds, a few metres behind her.

Like Cat, she had no idea what was going on between him and me. I hated lying to her as much as I hated lying to Cat. Sometimes, I just wanted to blurt out everything. Clear the air once and for all.

"Is something bothering you?" Eden asked. "You seem like you're on edge tonight. You know you can talk to me about anything, right?" She was perceptive. Sometimes I wondered how she hadn't guessed already.

"I know," I said lightly. "Everything is fine. I mean, it would have been better if the guys won, but there's always next time."

She gave me a doubtful look, but didn't push any further. Instead, she turned to lean her back against the bar and glanced around slowly. "I think this is the highest concentration of testosterone Opal Springs has ever seen."

I laughed. "You say that like it's a bad thing." I glanced around too, taking in the toned bodies of the Ghouls, the Fury, who came to commiserate with the hockey boys, and a handful of Ghosts, the local soccer team.

"It's like a dick buffet," Eden said with a grin.

"How many are you planning to feast on tonight?" I teased.

She shrugged. "Only the lucky ones."

I caught Oliver's eye before Cat came up to us, a brown haired guy in tow.

I froze. I knew that short hair and toned physique. The last time I saw him, it was dark, but I had no doubt it was him.

"Marley, I want to introduce you to Toby." Cat drew him over and all but pushed him in front of her.

Oliver followed, looking, of all things, amused.

"Um, hi," I said awkwardly.

"Hey there," he said in his American drawl. "Cat said you were cute, but she didn't say how cute." He offered his hand.

I took it and shook. A jolt of lightning passed all the way up my arm, right down into my core. I found my eyes locked on his, ready to drown in those depths.

"It's nice to meet you." I tried to sound smooth, but I probably squeaked.

"You two are already cute together, right Dad?" Cat asked.

Oliver hummed. "Yeah, adorable." He managed to contain a slight edge of pissed off.

Cat gave him a funny look, but hooked her arm in his and pulled him away. "Is your girlfriend coming?"

I didn't hear his answer as she pulled him away.

Toby arched an eyebrow at me.

"I'll leave you to it," Eden said. She gave me a quick hug and hurried away toward a group of our other friends.

Toby leaned his elbow on the bar beside me. "Wanna tell me what's going on?"

I sighed and took a big sip of my drink. "It's complicated."

"I can see that already." I waited for him to say it was none of his business, but he didn't.

"Not here," I said finally. I nodded towards the door that led out to the beer garden.

It should be almost empty out there on a cold night like this, even with the heaters going full blast. A handful of people were dotted around here or there, but we found a seat in a quiet corner and sat down.

"What you saw the other night," I started.

"It just *happened*?" he asked. "It was a one time thing for you to fuck your friend's father?"

I blinked at him. "You're very blunt."

"I'm from New York, we're not known for pulling any punches." He propped his elbow on the table.

"I can see that," I said dryly. I glanced around to make sure no one else was listening. "It's not a one time thing. It's been going on for a while."

"You seemed very comfortable with each other." He sipped his beer. "I take it your friend doesn't know. She seemed very interested in setting us up. An idea I wasn't averse to, personally. I'm still not." He raised an eyebrow at me. "A wise person once said if a guy keeps you as his dirty little secret, maybe he's not really into you."

I couldn't help bristling at his words, even though I'd thought them myself.

"Let me guess, this is where you say he's not like that." He smirked.

"You don't even know him," I snapped.

"You didn't tell me I'm wrong," Toby pointed out. He pointed a thick finger in the direction of my nose. "I can see the doubt on your face." He leaned in and looked at me intently. "If you were my woman and you were out here talking to some strange guy, I'd be right there, punching the crap out of him." He spread his hands out. "Where is he?"

I couldn't deny either his words, or the fact it was hot. I was a modern woman who could take care of myself, but his protective attitude made my clit throb a handful of times.

"It's complicated," I said. "It's not just about us. Cat would notice if he marched out here and punched the snot out of you."

"So what?" Toby asked. "Are you ashamed?"

"What? No." I squinted at him. "Of course I'm not, it's just— She's one of my best friends. She… She'd be pissed off if she knew about me and her father."

"Not much of a best friend if she doesn't want you to be happy," he said. "Not much of a daughter either, if you ask me."

"I wasn't asking you," I said bitterly. He hit too many nails on the head in a short amount of time. Everything he said, they were all things I'd considered before. Oliver and I should be able to do whatever we wanted without having to tiptoe around. Was this what he wanted? Maybe he got off on sneaking around like we were Romeo and Juliet or something. No thank you, given the way that ended.

He grinned, totally unapologetic and way too hot for his own good. "I've decided to make it my business. I like you. I think you deserve better than to be someone's side piece."

"What are you suggesting?" I asked.

"I'm suggesting we hang out sometime. If he sees what he's missing out on, great. If he doesn't, it's his loss and my gain." He sipped his beer and shrugged one shoulder.

"Do you always go after women so hard?" I asked.

"Only the gorgeous ones." His dark eyes drank me in slowly. "I figure, life is too short to wait around for it to happen. If I see what I want, I go after it. That's how I got where I am now. Goalie for a brand spanking new team."

"Why not stay in America and play?" I asked. "There's more money in it for you up there, isn't there?"

"There's more to life than money." His gaze lingered on my mouth. "I wanted a change. To see another part of the world. Experience it in a way I couldn't if I just came here for a vacay."

"That's very enlightened of you," I said. "I know people who've never left Opal Springs. Not me," I added quickly. "Just people who like to stay in their comfort zone." I wouldn't judge them for that. Comfort zones were nice places to be.

"Everywhere you go, there's people like that," he said. "The world would be boring if we were all the same. But that's not my jam."

"I guess that means you'll only stick around for a season or two," I said. For some reason, that thought made my heart sink a little.

"That depends if I have something to stick around for." He looked at me meaningfully.

"We've just met," I reminded him.

"Like I said, when I see something I want, I go after it. What I want is to get to know you better. I can tell you want that too." He wasn't lacking in the ego department.

"What if you're wrong?" I asked.

He chuckled. "I'm not. I know when a woman is feeling the same vibe I am, and you are. I bet if it wasn't for that Oliver dude, we'd be sneaking away already." He leaned in closer. "Maybe we should do that anyway. He doesn't seem in a hurry to take you out of here and get you naked."

His words sent a shiver up and down my spine.

"Like you said, we should get to know each other first," I said.

He was right though; if it wasn't for Oliver, I'd happily find a quiet corner and see how lickable his abs were.

I was tempted anyway. Oliver and I had never

talked about being exclusive. He'd never staked any particular claim to me or me to him. Maybe it would be better if I started seeing someone else. Someone I could spend time with in public, without having to worry about what other people thought. Someone I could sleep with without upsetting any of my friends. I could do worse than a guy like this.

"There's a lot of thought going on in your pretty little head," Toby said. "Are you picturing us both naked, my face between your legs?" He gave me a lopsided smile.

"Well I am *now*," I said. The image was an enticing one. I bet he knew what to do with his tongue. My panties were absolutely drenched. My clit very much wanted to be up close and personal with his mouth.

He looked smug. "I'm not going to apologise for putting that in your brain. Any time you want to experience the real thing, you only have to ask. I'd never turn down a woman in need, especially a beautiful one."

"How many times have you used that line on other women?" I asked.

He clicked his tongue. "So cynical. What makes you think I've used it on anyone else?"

I snorted softly. "Just a vibe I get. You seem like the kind of guy who gets around." I raised a hand. "Not that I'm judging. I'm just answering your question."

"I guess I deserved that." He grimaced, but only lightly. "I'd say I only practised so I could be perfect for you, but Australian girls don't seem to be impressed with shit like that. Come to think of it, American girls don't appreciate it much either. Lucky for everyone I prefer to be a straight shooter."

He sipped his beer and raised his glass to me. "I lick pussy because I like to. I like the taste and I like making women scream. I ain't apologising for that. I'm looking forward to making you scream."

"You think you can?" I challenged. I had no doubt he could, but I wasn't going to feed his already healthy ego if I could help it.

"I definitely can, all I need is for you to give me the chance."

"The chance for what?" Oliver asked. He stepped out the door into the beer garden and walked towards us, his expression tight, but clearly annoyed.

CHAPTER 5
OLIVER

I love my daughter. She's one of my proudest achievements. What I didn't appreciate was her pushing that guy at Marley. After everything Cat went through, I didn't want to hurt her, but my ability to respect her wishes wore thin.

Thinner still when Marley disappeared out to the beer garden with what's-his-name.

After seeing red for a long, drawn out moment, I knew it was the right thing for her to do. Anything else would raise suspicion from Cat and everyone else.

I had a feeling, by the way he kept watching me, that Shaw already suspected something was going on between us. Not much got past him. He didn't know anything for certain, or he would have told Cat. Unless he believed it was in her best interest not to say anything. In which case, it might only be a matter of time before he changed his mind.

"That assist from Easton was fucking awesome," Cruz was saying. "I couldn't have made that goal without him." He draped an arm over the other defenceman's shoulders and leaned into him. They were both with my daughter and also with each other. Both as arrogant as fuck.

Cat had forgiven them for giving her hell, but I had a longer memory than that. If either of them tried anything like that again, I'd make both of their lives hell. And short.

Although, I'd have to get in line behind her, Shaw and each other. They were all very protective of her. Fuck knew she was good at standing up for herself.

"Shame you didn't get more goals," Saxon Davies said as he stepped past the table. He stopped to smirk. "Opal Springs doesn't need more than one premier sports team anyway."

"Fuck off, Davies," Cruz snarled. "There's plenty of room in this town for more local heroes like us. Stop trying to hog the spotlight."

"He's just trying to compensate for having a tiny cock," Easton said.

Saxon laughed. "That's it, keep projecting. I know how big my cock is."

"So do half the women in town," Cat said.

That made him smirk even harder. "Only the discerning ones. The rest end up with losers like these guys." He gestured towards Cat's boyfriends.

"Did I mention, fuck off?" Cruz said. "We already

know which one of you is the evil twin, you don't need to keep showing off."

"You said 'talented, good-looking twin,' wrong," Saxon said. "No wonder my brother likes playing with you losers. He's in good company."

"Is that jealousy I hear in your tone?" Easton asked. "You weren't good enough at ice hockey to play, and had to stick to football?"

"In your fucking dreams," Saxon sneered. "We don't have to wear all that padding like we're a pack of princesses. Rugby is a real man's game."

I sat back and listened to them fling insults back and forth. As a doctor, I'd seen my share of injuries from both sports. They were rough as hell, and a very good way to lose your teeth. I was never much into team sports anyway. Once upon a time, when I was their age, I made the Winter Olympics in speed skating. Cat inherited the love of the sport from me. If not for an accident, I might have taken out the gold medal. Those days were a long time ago. I hardly thought about them anymore.

"If you ever get tired of these idiots, look me up," Saxon said to Cat.

She snorted. "Not if you were the last guy in town."

"You say that now, but you might change your mind." He kissed the air, his eyes on her before turning and walking away.

"He's such a dickhead," Easton said. "I'm starting to think he got tackled a few too many times."

"To be fair, he was always a dickhead," Cruz said. "If it wasn't us threatening other kids for their lunch for lunch money, it was him."

"He looks more like the sort of guy who'd tell the teacher," Shaw said.

The other guys laughed.

"That sounds more like it," Easton said.

I tuned in and out again and looked towards the beer garden. Marley was still sitting opposite that guy, deep in conversation. The whole time they'd been sitting there, he'd gotten closer and closer. I'd recognised him as the person who walked upon us beside Marley's car, just after we'd fucked. When I first saw him, I'd expected him to say something to Cat. Thank fuck he hadn't. Doing that would have lost him teeth too.

I let my mind drift to the memory of Marley's pussy around my cock. I couldn't get enough of being inside her. I didn't care about the difference in our ages, we got along better than I did with anyone my own age. She was smart, sweet and had the most incredible pussy I'd ever had the privilege to know.

I'd fallen for her long before we were ever intimate. I suspected she had no idea how deep my feelings for her went. Losing her would be as devastating as it was when we lost Cat and Bree's mother. Sooner or later, I'd have to officially stake my claim.

I squinted. Toby had moved even closer. I'd seen a

man make his move often enough to recognise one from a distance.

"Excuse me." I rose to my feet and strode away before they had time to respond.

"All you need to do is give me a chance," Toby was saying.

"A chance for what?" I asked before I could stop myself.

Toby glanced over at me, looked me up and down and then back to my face. "That's between me and her, old man. She's tired of being treated like she's nothing. Just someone to use to get your dick wet."

I didn't rise to the bait. Instead, I turned to Marley. "Is he bothering you? It seems to me like he's outstayed his welcome."

The smile I gave to him wasn't pleasant. The double meaning to my words should be obvious. If he didn't think I could get him deported, he could think again. I had contacts neither of my daughters, nor Marley, had any clue about. I could have him on the next plane back to New York before he could blink. With or without an injury; that was up to him.

"He's not bothering me," Marley said. "He was keeping me company." Judging by the pink on her cheeks, he was doing a lot more than that.

"Is that what you want?" I wasn't going to let her end things between us, not just like that. Not without a fight from me.

On the other hand, I'd seen how Cat was with her

three guys. If Marley wanted a similar relationship, I'd let her do that. She deserved to have all of her needs met.

She glanced over at Toby, then back at me. "Toby, can you give us a few minutes, please?"

He narrowed his eyes at me in warning. In warning. As if I'd ever do anything to hurt her. Arrogant prick.

Finally, he rose. "I'll get us another round of drinks."

How big of him. As if I didn't make more money than he did.

He was barely more than a step or two away before I sat in the seat he'd just vacated.

"I know Cat tried to set you up, but you don't need to spend time with anyone you don't want to just to make her happy." I wanted to pull her into my lap and hold her close. I wanted to slip my hands up under her top and pinch her nipples. My balls were aching just thinking about it.

"But I have to stay away from you in public to make her happy," Marley said bitterly. "How is that any different? I'm tired of sneaking around in the shadows. I'm sick of lying to her. And Eden. I think we need to either come clean or end it."

"He really got into your head didn't he?" I asked.

She sat back and gaped at me. "Yes. No." She exhaled heavily with frustration. "I was thinking all of this before I spoke to him. Maybe it's a good thing. He's interested in me and doesn't want to hide it."

"So go out with him," I said.

She gaped at me again. "What? Did you just tell me to go out with him?"

"Yes, I did," I said evenly. "I see no reason why you can't see us both. When the time comes, we can explain everything to Cat. In the meantime, you should go out and enjoy yourself."

"Are you ending it?" She frowned.

I leaned in close. "No. I am not, nor will I *ever* end my relationship with you. But you can have a relationship with me and someone else, if that's what you choose. Including a physical relationship."

The thought of Toby touching her made me want to stab him in the eyeball with a scalpel, but this was about more than me. I couldn't give her everything she wanted, not until Cat had her baby. I wouldn't risk my grandchild if I could help it. Not unless it meant losing Marley forever.

"You're okay with me fucking Toby?" She blinked a few times and shook her head. "This is…"

"It really is," I agreed. "Just until Cat has the baby. I swear to you right now, the moment that happens, I'll tell her everything. You and I can be free to see each other wherever and however we want."

"I want that," she said softly. "I'll hold you to that. Are you really sure you don't mind me seeing someone else?"

"I mind," I said. "But that's my problem. If he hurts you, I'll rearrange his face, but your happiness is more important to me than my ego. I'll leave the arrogance to the hockey players. And the rugby players."

"The soccer players have egos too," Marley pointed out. "It seems to go with the territory."

"Fortunately, us doctors are humble," I said jokingly. I wasn't humble, I just kept my arrogance in check slightly better. Maybe that came with getting older.

She snorted. "Very humble, Doctor Ryan."

I smiled. "Don't you forget it, Marley-Jane Hammond." I loved the way her name sounded on my tongue. Almost as good as she tasted.

"I wish I could fast forward to the day she has her baby." Marley's expression was wistful. "Because we get to be together and I get a baby to play with. I have a few other friends with babies, but none are close to me like she is."

"You're looking forward to being a step-grandmother?" I teased.

Her eyes widened. "That makes me sound old."

I chuckled. "I'm not old and I'll be the grandfather." After a moment I added, "If we had a child, they'd be younger than their nibling?"

The flush was back on her cheeks. That was what I thought.

"Nibling?" she asked.

"Like niece or nephew, but gender neutral," I said. "I have no idea what the sex of the baby is."

Knowing my daughter and her boyfriends, the child

would be on ice skates before they could walk, regardless. If Cat had a girl, she might end up playing professional women's ice hockey someday. Hopefully, that would be a thing by then. If it wasn't, she'd probably find a way to make it one. Stubborn women were plentiful in my family.

"The baby is bound to be cute though," Marley said. "With Cat for a mother, how could they not? Not to mention having you for a grandfather."

"Knowing my luck, the baby will look just like whichever of those guys contributed his sperm to their creation," I said. "Then they won't be so pretty." According to my daughter, they were all gorgeous, but I wasn't even going to try to look at them that way. That would be about a billion different kinds of wrong. At least.

"Don't pretend you won't love that baby just as much as the rest of us," Marley said.

I would, but I saw the longing in her eyes. The question was, what did I do about it?

CHAPTER 6

MARLEY

"Did I give you long enough?" Toby drawled. He eyed Oliver, who slid out of the seat and gestured for him to reclaim it.

"Yes, you did," Oliver said for us both. He stood almost toe to toe with the goalie. Toby only had a couple of centimetres on him.

"Marley and I have come to an understanding. She'll explain it. How in, or out, you are is up to you and her. Mostly her. If you hurt her in any way, you can kiss your hockey career goodbye. Understood?"

Toby smirked. "As long as we understand that if you do the same, you can kiss your medical license good-bye." He didn't flinch.

Neither did Oliver. He smiled, but it wasn't a pleasant one. "I know you think you're a badass by threatening me, but I could fuck you up way worse than you could fuck me up." Before Toby could say anything more, he turned and walked back into the pub.

Toby watched him with a frown creasing his brow before he slipped back into the chair.

"His bark is worse than his bite," I said. My panties were even wetter after watching them talk to each other like that. Apparently possessive and growly was more my thing than I thought.

Toby shook his head slowly. "I doubt that. I think he meant every word." He placed his beer on the table and lounged back in his chair, his frown smoothing out. "So, you were going to fill me in on something?"

I explained the conversation between me and Oliver as briefly as I could. Toby listened, looking more and more surprised.

"Your boyfriend has given you permission to go out with me, even fuck me? What happens when you're free to see each other openly? When everyone knows, instead of you screwing around behind their backs?" He certainly didn't pull any punches.

When I was done wincing at his wording, I said, "That's up to us. If we like each other and want to keep seeing each other, we can. But this is getting way ahead of ourselves. We haven't even been out on a date. I might go out with you and not like you."

Toby smiled. "That's not possible. I'm very likeable." He leaned forward and propped his elbows on the table. "I can promise you this: once I fuck you, you won't forget me. You won't want to. When I slide my cock into your pussy, I'm going to claim you. There won't be any going back from that." He nodded once and sat back again.

Holy shit, that was hot.

I swallowed hard. "You seem very sure of that."

"I am," he said. "I was sure the moment I saw you. We could go somewhere now and I could prove it to you, but it's too soon."

I suppressed a small stab of disappointment. "It is?"

"Yes, it is. I want you to fall for me first," he said.

"You seem very sure I will," I said. "You know Oliver and I—"

"I don't care about him," Toby said. "This is between you and me. I understand you're going to see him too, but love isn't a pie. There aren't a finite number of pieces before you run out. You can care about him and me at the same time. I have big enough balls to share."

I'd very much like to see his balls, but I'd also like to get to know him before I jumped in with both feet.

"What are you proposing?" I asked. He seemed to have a firm idea in his mind. If I liked what I heard, I'd let him take the lead.

"I'm proposing we go out on a date," he said. "It seems to be what everyone wants, including you and me. You want that?"

He phrased it as a question, but I suspected he was making a statement.

"Something you should know about me," I said slowly. "I don't let myself get pushed into situations I don't want to be a part of. I don't like hiding Oliver and me from the rest of the world, but being with him is worth it. I wouldn't date you just to make him and Cat happy if I didn't want to."

"Would you date me to make me happy?" he asked, a smile tugging at the side of his mouth.

I leaned forward far enough to give him an eyeful of cleavage, smiled and said, "No. I'd date you for one reason and only one reason. To make *me* happy."

"I like a woman who knows how to stand up for herself," he said. "It's hot as fuck. No wonder Oliver is into you."

"Now you agree he's into me," I teased.

"I saw the look on the prick's face," Toby said. "I know when a guy's head over heels for a woman. That particular one is as gone as anyone I've ever seen. It must be killing him to keep you a secret. But his loss is my gain. It gives me time to claim what's mine."

"You seem very sure I fall under that description," I said.

He smiled. "You don't seem in a hurry to deny it."

"Why me?" I said. "I know Opal Springs isn't that big, but there's plenty of single women around. My friend Eden, for one."

"Is she the one with purple hair I just saw in the middle of a centre sandwich near the pool table?" he asked. "If she's not spoken for, she soon will be. Lucky Mitch and Jagger get along so well. Otherwise they'd be punching the shit out of each other right now."

I glanced towards the door. I couldn't see Eden, which was probably for the best. I wasn't sure I really needed to see her in a sandwich with the Ghoul's centre and alternate. I knew she had a thing for them both, but I didn't realise it had progressed. Good for her.

"Yeah, that's her," I said. "They're still lots of single women in Opal Springs. So, why me?" I wasn't fishing for compliments. I was genuinely curious as to why a guy who barely knew me seemed so sure we had some sort of future.

"Why not you?" he asked. He rubbed a hand over the back of his neck. "I saw you standing by the bar and I said to myself, 'Tobias Glover, that looks like a woman who'd be perfect with your hand around her throat.' So here we are. Let me take you out on a date and prove my instinct wasn't wrong."

My face heated. I could almost feel his fingers around my neck, squeezing while he drove his cock into me. I couldn't deny the physical attraction, there was plenty of that. I considered whether I really wanted to complicate my life more than it already was. I mean, sooner or later Oliver and I would be out in the open. Wasn't he enough man for me?

On the other hand, I was curious about Toby. Maybe he was right and we were meant to be together. It certainly wouldn't hurt to try.

"Yes," I said. "I'll go out on a date with you, just to see if anything might happen between us. If it doesn't, then no harm, no foul. We'll get on with our lives."

He took my hand and traced circles around my palm with the pad of his thumb. His touch felt like a flint, striking sparks that threatened to burst into flames.

"I have a lot to prove, but I will prove it to you," he said. "You and I are as inevitable as the sunrise."

"Until you go back to America," I said.

"I won't go back if you ask me to stay." He pressed his lips together. "Give it time. You'll see."

"Where are you going to take me?" I asked. "On our date, I mean."

He smiled at the inadvertent innuendo. "If I told you, it wouldn't be a surprise. Do you like surprises?"

"I like *pleasant* surprises," I said.

He chuckled. "No one likes unpleasant surprises. Don't worry, I'll take you somewhere you'll never forget."

"Look at you two looking all cosy." Zane Bradbury and Elliott Quinn were both forwards for the Ghouls. I didn't know either of them well, but they both carried strong asshole vibes. More so than Cruz and Easton ever had. Cole Davies was right behind them.

Zane stopped at the table to leer down at my cleavage. "Is this prick bothering you?" He jerked his thumb towards Toby. "How's about we save you from him? We can show you a good time, can't we, fellas?"

"Fucking right we can," Elliott agreed. He actually stepped up to me and cupped to the side of my neck with his large hand. "Come on, babe."

I slapped his hand away. "I'm not your babe. Fuck off."

"Leave her alone," Cole said softly. "She's clearly not interested."

Zane turned to him. "You going soft, Davies? Since when do we ask?"

"Since you don't want your teeth knocked down your throat," Toby growled. He rose to his feet, his face pink with anger. "I suggest you gentlemen back the fuck off."

Zane looked me up and down with disgust. "Bitch probably doesn't put out anyway. Waste of fucking time." He turned and stomped away.

Elliott gave me a similar look before following his friend.

"They're drunk," Cole said apologetically. "I was trying to get them to go home."

"Good idea," Toby said. "Before they get their asses handed to them."

Cole gave him a nod, and me a half a smile before he trudged after the other two players.

Toby waited until they were all gone to sink back into his seat. "Fucking meatheads."

"We know who the good twin is," I said. Cole's brother would have joined in, not tried to get them to back off.

Toby snorted softly. "Looks to me like a good cop, bad cop act. He's probably just as big a prick as his brother."

"Maybe," I said thoughtfully.

I wasn't sure about that; Cole seemed nice, but it was possible he was a good actor. He seemed genuinely annoyed at his teammates' behaviour. I made a note to thank him for sticking up for me when I saw him next. Hopefully I wouldn't need intervention like that again anytime soon. The team had worked too long and too hard to be brought into disrepute by a couple of guys after too many beers.

"I'll pick you up tomorrow at six o'clock," Toby said, breaking through my thoughts. "Wear something nice but not too fancy."

I could almost hear him thinking that whatever I wore, he was looking forward to seeing it lying on the floor. So was I, but there was no hurry. We might go on a ton of dates before we even kissed. Or we might go on one and hate each other.

In spite of how adamant he was that we were meant to be together, I'd wait and see. The last thing I wanted to do was make assumptions and be disappointed. Having physical attraction to someone was great, but if we had nothing in common, there'd be no point in pursuing a relationship.

Although, we already agreed on one thing: Zane and Elliott were meatheads. It didn't surprise me at all they'd act like that towards me, or any other woman. They probably didn't get turned down very often. I smiled to myself.

"I see you're thinking about me," Toby said.

I laughed softly and shook my head. "I was thinking Elliott and Zane are dickheads, but if that's what you want to think, then go ahead."

"I much prefer to think you were thinking about me," Toby agreed. "I know you will be all day tomorrow, right up until our date."

"Maybe I will and maybe I won't," I said lightly. I probably would. He had me intrigued. Even if we weren't compatible, I'd probably have a good time wherever he decided to take me.

CHAPTER 7
MARLEY

Toby regarded me as I slipped into the leather seat of his Maserati. For someone who said there was more to life than money, he had a fancy car.

"What?" I raised my eyebrows at him.

"You look beautiful." He handed me an envelope.

"What's this?" I asked.

"Open it," he said.

I shrugged and slid my nail under the back of the envelope to open it. Inside was a card, folded in two.

"Read it," he said.

I opened the card. Written inside, were the words;

A place for all the stories

"It's a clue," he said. "So you can figure out where I'm taking you."

"I didn't pick you for a romantic," I said.

He flashed me a panty-melting smile. "I'm many things, including that. Did you think I was just some meathead too?"

"I barely know you," I said. "You could be both of those things."

He chuckled. "Fair call." He nodded towards the card in my hand. "Any guesses?"

I looked back at the words, read them again. "It could be a building with lots of stories. There's a few of those in Opal Springs." Nothing above ten floors, and most not even that. The town wasn't big enough to be called a city, not yet.

"It might be," he said.

I glanced over at him. "But it's not?"

"You tell me," he said. "Any other ideas?"

"It could be the Opal Springs library," I said slowly.

"Getting warmer, but not the library," he said.

"Not the library," I said thoughtfully. "In that case, drive three blocks in that direction, then turn right."

"If you're sure." He turned the engine on and peeled the sports car away from the curb.

"I'm not sure, but I suppose we'll find out." I turned the card over to search for other clues, but there weren't any. If I was wrong, I didn't know what else to suggest, I was out of guesses.

He turned right on Perkins Street and drove slowly. "Say when."

I said nothing for a minute or two, then pointed off to the side. "When. Here."

He pulled the car into an empty space in front of the bookshop. "Here?" He had the perfect poker face. I couldn't tell if I was right or not.

"You tell me," I said.

Finally, his lips curved upward into a smile. "You're right so far."

"We're going on a date to the bookshop?" I asked.

Who was this guy and how did he know one of my favourite places in town?

"I asked Cat, and she said you like to read. I figured maybe you could pick out a few books." He shrugged.

I wondered when he talked to her, but I'd never say no to more books.

Grinning, I pushed out of the car and stepped out. He offered me his arm and led me through the open doors.

"Good morning." Amanda, the owner, stood behind the desk, which was weighed down with displays full of bookmarks and book themed stickers. "Here's your next clue."

She held out an envelope the same as the one Toby gave me.

"I feel like I'm on some sort of game show." I took the envelope and smiled my thanks. "I don't have to eat any disgusting food to get the next clue, do I?"

"I wouldn't do that to you," Toby said. "Not on the first date. That's second date stuff."

I batted him lightly on the chest with one end of the envelope before tearing it open. The next clue read,

Where the heart takes you

"The romance section?" I asked. I knew exactly where that was. That was my favourite section. I especially loved that Amanda stocked titles from indie authors, as well as those who were with traditional publishers. The combination was practically perfect.

I headed through the shop, inhaling the smell of books, before I stopped at the extensive romance section. It consisted of one whole wall and both sides of four shelves, which reached to the ceiling. Step stools were scattered around the place so nothing was out of reach.

"Hmmm, if you spoke to Cat for long enough, she would have told you my favourite books are poly romance." The irony of me reading about reverse harems wasn't lost on me. There was something about the celebration of women's sexuality, and a group of hot guys that did it for me.

Like before, Toby's face was unreadable. He leaned against the end of a shelf and crossed his arms over his burly chest. He offered the slightest hint of an eyebrow arch, but that was it. I had to figure this out on my own.

Never let it be said that Marley-Jane Hammond backed down from a challenge. I pushed my glasses back up my nose and started to search through the books.

I slid out each one to check book by book. I tucked

the ones I hadn't read yet under my arm. I might as well do some shopping while I was here.

As I pulled out the fourth, Toby stepped over to take the stack from me. "I'll hold these for you."

I glanced over at him. "That's the five words every woman wants to hear."

He grinned. "Along with, 'Every woman needs more books.'"

I laughed softly. "You're so right." He was getting hotter by the minute. And so was I.

I looked through several more books, handing him another three. When I pulled out the one beside a rock star romance, I found another envelope. I wasted no time opening this one.

Lunch is served

I glanced over at Toby. He held the pile of books in one arm and offered me his other. "Come with me."

I grabbed another book to add to the pile, then another for good measure, before I took his arm and let him lead me to the small coffee shop in the rear of the bookshop.

The place was empty except for us. A crisp, blue tablecloth was draped over one of the tables. Plates containing hamburgers and chips sat waiting, the smell enticing.

"I hope you don't mind burgers." He placed the pile

of books on the counter and pulled out his card to pay for them.

"I love burgers," I said. I didn't mind fancy food, but I preferred simple, with all the flavours and delicious carbohydrates.

He placed the bag of books down beside me and gestured for me to sit and start eating.

"When did you have time to organise all of this?" I asked.

He shrugged. "I had some help." He picked up a chip and waved it in Amanda's direction. "I just wrote the clues."

"But you thought up all of this," I said. "That's the important part."

"Would your doctor friend do this for you?" Toby asked before popping the chip in his mouth. "Mmm, that's a good fry."

"I'm sure he would if he thought of it," I said. "And if…"

"If you didn't have to sneak around?" There he went, being blunt again.

"That too," I agreed reluctantly. "It's nice to do something out in public."

"I noticed you like doing it in public." He gave me a sly smile.

I picked up a chip and threw it at him. "That wasn't what I meant and you know it."

He caught the chip and ate it. Of course he did; he wasn't a goalie for nothing. "But you do, don't you? You like the thrill of potentially being caught. There's no shame in it, I like it myself. Although…"

"Although, what?" I prompted. "You can't say all of that and then leave me hanging."

He picked up his burger, made a face at the beetroot before he slipped it out and dropped it onto his plate. "The hell is that doing on a burger?"

I laughed. "Welcome to Australia. You didn't answer the question."

"I didn't, did I?" He bit into his burger and chewed. He swallowed and nodded his approval. "The rest is pretty good without that weird pink shit on there."

I shook my head at him and ate mine, beetroot and all, and waited for him to elaborate. If he wanted to.

Halfway through his burger, he stopped and said, "I've been known to dabble in a bit of exhibitionism."

"Fucking in front of other people?" I asked. My heart raced a little faster.

"Yeah," he said lightly. "And being naked for money. Before I went pro, I had a JustPeens channel, where I used to do a roundup of the week's hockey games, while I was naked. No one saw my face, it was from here down." He gestured from his throat to his feet.

"You'd be surprised how many people are interested in hockey when it's presented like that. I might have even converted a few folks to actually watching the game."

It took me a while to process all of that. "You had a

channel on JustPeens? Is it still there? I mean, asking out of curiosity."

"You can see the real thing anytime you want," he said. "For the record, no, it's not. That's the kind of thing the NHL prefers we not do. The AIHL too, probably."

"How many followers did you have?" I asked.

"You wanna know how many people saw my dick?" he asked. "Lots. But looking and touching are very different beasts." He finished his burger and wiped his hands on the napkin beside his plate. "Does that scare you off?"

"That you know enough about hockey to have lots of people follow you and listen?" I said. "No, there are worse things a guy can do."

Toby chuckled. "Yeah, it was all about the hockey. I'm glad you can look past my abundant knowledge of the sport. It'd be a total drag otherwise."

"I'm sure it would." I reached for my own napkin and wiped my fingers. "The other stuff doesn't worry me either. I mean, it's your dick, and you said you needed the money. A guy's gotta do what a guy's gotta do, right?"

"So it wouldn't bother you if I fucked in front of a camera?" he asked.

"You were a porn star too?" I asked.

He smiled. "No, just curious what your reaction would be if I was."

"I have better things to do than judge you," I said. "I

have a funny feeling the NHL would have judged you a lot more harshly."

"Amen to that." He grimaced. "I'd still do it, but not for public consumption. Just for us to enjoy."

"That's something I might need to work up to," I said. "Is that what you meant by exhibitionism?"

"Some," he agreed. "Parties have been known to get wild once in a while. I'm not shy about what I do or who I do it with, or who I do it in front of, as long as what happens at a party stays at the party. Which can be tricky, once the public starts to know your name."

"Paparazzi taking photos of that wouldn't be good," I guessed.

"Not for me and or anyone I was with," he agreed.

I took another moment to process his words. "Women and men?" He hadn't specified, leaving me to wonder if he meant both, or either.

"Yeah. Is that a problem?" he asked. For the first time, he looked uncertain. Like maybe I'd get up and walk away because he'd fucked other men.

I couldn't really be unruffled knowing about his JustPeens past, and then judge him for this. Besides, I was a firm believer that love was love.

"Not even a little bit," I replied. "If you want to be with someone else and me, I'm all for it."

"I'm not interested in another woman, but maybe another guy," he said slowly. "But I'm not going to sneak around behind your back. If any of this comes to pass, it happens out in the open. Maybe literally." He grinned.

"Agreed." I took his hand and squeezed. Life might be about to get a whole lot more complicated.

CHAPTER 8
MARLEY

"Then we took a walk around Opal Springs and we talked for hours," I said. "He told me all about the team he played for in New York and how he liked the change of pace from that."

"It sounds like you like him." Eden handed us mugs; tea for Cat, coffee for me.

I nodded my thanks and wrapped my fingers around the mug, savouring the warmth that seeped through the porcelain.

"I do like him," I said. "He's interesting. And hot when he's telling other guys to stop being dickheads." And warning Oliver, but I couldn't say that out loud.

"Will you be seeing him again?" Cat asked. She sat back on Eden's couch, trying to get comfortable.

"Probably." I sat beside her. "I had a good time and I think he did too." He hadn't asked me out again, but he'd spoken like second and third dates were inevitable.

"It's good that you're seeing someone." Cat took a sip of her tea and half closed her eyes as she savoured the taste. She preferred coffee, but she loved tea almost as much. "I was starting to worry about you a little bit."

"You were?" I frowned. "Why?"

"It can't be healthy spending all of your time with my father," she said. "I love him to bits, but everyone needs a break from work. I know how driven he can be. The late hours you've been putting in because of him are a lot. If you want me to talk to him, to make sure he's not working you too hard—"

"No," I said quickly. "He's not working me too hard at all." Not in the way she meant. A lot of those late afternoons, we were taking time to be together, not because he had taken on extra patients. I wanted to tell her that, but I glanced down at her belly and bit my tongue. If I said something now and the stress hurt the baby, neither she nor Oliver would forgive me.

No, it was getting harder, but it would have to wait. I suppressed a surge of frustration, and the hint of resentment that came with it. I was hating this more and more by the day, but I had no choice at all. Our time would come. It had to.

I cleared my throat, and my thoughts with it. "I love my job. I don't mind working all the hours Oliv— Doctor Ryan gives me."

Surely I was as transparent as a window that had just been cleaned. How did they not both see right through me? They trusted me to be honest with them and I wasn't. I felt like shit for continuing to lie to them both.

"Cat's right," Eden said. "It's good that you're seeing someone." She glanced at us both, uncertain as to whether she should continue. "For a while there, I got the feeling Oliver was interested in you."

My laugh in response was uncomfortably high-pitched. "What gave you that impression?"

"Seriously?" Cat pulled a face. "Can we not talk about my father like that? Yuck. There's no way he'd be interested in Marley or anyone else our age. No offence," she added, offering me a small smile.

Offence taken, but I forced a smile back. "Why not? I mean, people get together with people older than them all the time. Don't tell me you don't believe love is love."

"It's not about the age gap," Cat said. "It's about him being my father and your boss. It would be all kinds of wrong. Imagine if things went bad. You'd have to find another job. You said it yourself, you love what you do. You wouldn't want to risk that, would you?"

"What if it didn't go bad?" I asked. "What if we were perfect for each other and destined to last forever?" As far as I was concerned, that was exactly what we were.

"I don't really see any point in thinking about it." Cat tucked some strands of red hair behind her ear. "You said you like Toby and you're going to see him again. He sounds perfect for you. A guy who buys you books has to be a keeper, right?"

"Absolutely," Eden agreed. "Does he have a brother?"

"Do you need one?" I asked teasingly. "I heard something about you being in the middle of a centre sandwich the other night." I raised my eyebrows at her, happy to have the conversation focus on someone else for now.

Eden smiled. "Maybe I was."

"And?" I gave her a 'tell us more' gesture with my fingers.

"And we played pool, had a few drinks and some laughs, then we went home," she said.

"Alone?" Cat asked.

Eden sighed. "They had early training in the morning. When we get together, it's amazing, but I don't know if either of them want more than fun here or there."

I grimaced. "That sucks. It sounds like you need to meet someone new too. There was no shortage of hot guys in O'Reilly's the other night." Some were even nice.

"Both Elliott and Zane hit on me," Eden said. "I was tempted to go home with one of them, just to see what Mitch and Jagger would do. But then I realised something."

"You have taste and dignity?" Cat asked.

"Exactly." Eden laughed. "My clit was so sad. She has neither taste nor dignity, apparently. She just wants to have a good time."

"It sounds like she's ready to lead you astray," I remarked. Not that I could talk. Mine had led me astray for quite a while now. Although, there was more to my relationship with Oliver than sex. With Toby there wasn't even sex, not yet. When he took me home, he only gave me a kiss on the cheek. One I could still feel, like a lingering warmth on my skin.

I could easily have taken him inside and fucked his brains out, but where was the hurry? My vibrator got a workout instead.

"Maybe I should let her," Eden said. "We're only talking about orgasms here. Is it possible I'm being too fussy?"

"There's no such thing as too fussy," Cat said. "Do what feels right. Don't worry about what other people say."

"That's good advice," I said. "Never let anyone stand in the way of your happiness or your orgasms."

Wasn't I doing just that? I couldn't wait until Cat had her baby. I just hoped like hell she didn't hate my guts when Oliver and I told her what was going on. She and I had been friends since we were kids. I didn't want to lose her. I was terrified she'd insist on Oliver choosing between me and her.

No matter how much he cared about me, there was no way he wouldn't choose his daughter, especially with a baby involved.

Eden might choose Cat's side as well. When the dust

settled, I could lose everything. The idea was absolutely terrifying.

"Are you okay?" Eden asked me. "You look pale."

I blinked at her a couple of times. "I'm a blonde, I'm supposed to be pale."

"Paler than usual," she said, laughing on an exhale. "You seem worried about something."

"I'm fine," I said. "Everything is just perfect." So many things were so far from perfect it wasn't funny. "It was disappointing that the Ghouls lost the other night, but they'll win next time."

I sat back while Cat told us all about her guys' reaction to losing and their determination not to be beaten again. Toby said many of the same things, with the additional frustration of having let goals get past him. Even if the team didn't blame him for the loss, he blamed himself.

I'd reminded him a team wasn't just one player, but I understood his frustration. They badly wanted to win and they hadn't. But it was only one game. The first of many.

"What do you think?" Eden asked.

I frowned. "What about?" I'd checked out for a minute or two. Now, they were both looking at me expectantly.

"Do you think Nutella and Vegemite would taste good together?" Eden asked.

I thought she was serious until she surrendered to the smile that pushed at the corners of her mouth.

"First of all, absolutely not. Secondly, what were you really asking? I was away with the fairies for a moment."

"We could tell," Cat said. "I was just saying it would be nice to get a few people together at the old rink for a recreational skate. I won't have much time for it when the baby is born. Are you in?"

"Sure." I shrugged. I was nowhere near as good at ice-skating as she was, but I enjoyed it now and again. "Maybe Toby will come along."

"Definitely ask him," she agreed. "I might see if Dad will come too. He still enjoys getting his skates on from time to time. Now the team isn't practising at Rhonda's rink any more, she's going to need more people there to make up for the loss of revenue."

"If you're going to skate, I doubt you could keep your father away," I said. "He's very protective of you and that baby you're carrying. If anything happened to you, he'd want to be there to help you."

"That sounds like Dad." Cat grimaced. "He's the definition of overprotective. I suppose it comes with the territory of being a doctor and a father."

"You'll be exactly the same when your little one is born," Eden said. "So will those guys of yours."

"If they had their way, the baby would be skating already." Cat rubbed her belly. "They've already bought tiny hockey sticks and pucks. And the smallest sized jerseys they could get in Ghouls colours. If they had their way, the baby's name would be Hockey Ryan."

Eden and I both laughed.

"They might be the tiniest bit obsessed," I said.

Cat held up her fingers, slightly apart. "A tiny bit. But they're all going to adore this baby. I can't wait until they're born. It's been a long time since I've seen my own feet without a lot of effort."

"That baby is going to be very loved," I said. "A wonderful mother and three doting fathers."

"And if Easton gets his way, another sibling shortly after." Cat pulled a face. "He loves me being pregnant."

I'd seen them together, his hands on her bump. The way he looked at her and her growing belly, like he worshipped both of them, was sweet. From what she'd told me, they were barely together when he first told her he wanted her to get pregnant. Who was I to shame him for his kink?

"You look adorable." I couldn't help a slight stab of envy. Just a little one, because life was already complicated enough as it was.

"I feel like a giant manatee," she said. "But it's sweet of you to say so. You will be babysitting for me, right?" She turned her sweetest smile on both of us.

"Just try to stop us," Eden said. "Both of us are looking forward to it. I never want to have my own children, but I like spending small amounts of time with other people's. As long as I can give the baby back and walk away at the end of the day, I'm content."

As long as I'd known Eden, she'd said she didn't want to be a mother. I supported her a hundred percent, but I didn't feel the same way about myself. Someday, when the time was right, I wanted babies. Fuck only knew when the time would be right though.

"I'll pencil you in for the second round of babysitting duties," Cat said. "I think my father will be first in line for that. I always got the impression he would have liked more than two. He's going to absolutely dote on this little one." She patted her belly.

He definitely would. I wondered how he'd feel about him and I having a baby together. That was another question I had no answers for right now. Yet another thing that was on hold until the right time.

CHAPTER 9

MARLEY

"Is that the third puck related injury this week, or the fourth?" I placed Oliver's coffee down in front of him and leaned my hip against the edge of the desk. "I've lost count."

He chuckled and finished typing whatever he was typing before leaning back in his chair and picking up his mug. "Half the kids in Opal Springs want to be ice hockey players now. The other half can't seem to decide between rugby injuries or soccer ones."

None of the injuries looked major to me, just a bump to the head or the occasional broken arm.

"Isn't that how it goes?" I asked. "Half want to be ice hockey players and the other half want to be *with* ice hockey players."

He hummed indeterminately. "Which one are you? How did your date with Toby go?"

He tried to keep his voice light, but I knew him well

enough to know he was slightly on edge. Not entirely certain of this agreement.

"It was nice," I said. "We're going out again on Sunday night."

"Did you sleep with him?" Oliver asked.

"Did you take lessons in being blunt from him?" I placed my mug down and sighed. "No, I didn't. We decided not to rush."

"Good." Oliver nodded slowly.

I watched his expression for a few moments. "Is this where you tell me you've changed your mind? You don't want to share?"

"I haven't changed my mind, but the idea of him touching you still makes me stabby." He smiled faintly.

"You can't go around stabbing people," I said. "Especially when you agreed to—"

He rose and grabbed my arm to pull me toward him. "I know what I agreed to. I also know how I feel about you and I don't want you to get hurt. I wish we could be together all the time. With or without Toby or whoever catches your eye."

I leaned into him, my face pressed against his chest. "I want that too. I feel like we've waited forever. I understand why we have to keep waiting, but it's hard."

He chuckled and pressed his growing erection against my leg. "It always is around you, Marley-Jane."

"I've noticed that about you, Oliver John Ryan," I teased.

"What can I say, you're a fucking gorgeous woman,

who I can't get enough of." He nuzzled his face into my hair.

"Which reminds me, I need a new prescription for my birth control," I said.

"I'll fix it up." He ran his hands down my back, to my ass, picked me up and placed me on the top of the desk. "In the meantime, it's time for you to have a thorough examination."

"Is that right?" I asked teasingly.

"Definitely." He slid his hands up my skirt, over my thighs. He traced light circles on the insides as he went, inching up every centimetre of my skin. "You know what they say, Doctor knows best."

"I haven't heard that one before," I said. I placed my hands on the desk behind me and leaned back, letting my legs drop open wider.

"Really? I'll have to say it more often." He pushed my skirt up to my hips and ran the pad of his thumb across the gusset of my panties. His caress sent a jolt of electricity all the way through me. He always knew exactly how to touch me to turn me into a needy pool of jelly.

"Or you could just not talk at all?" I suggested.

"Oh?" He glanced up at me. "You can think of something better for me to do with my mouth?"

"Definitely." I rolled my hips, rubbing my pussy against his hand.

"Whatever the woman wants." He took hold of the waistband of my panties and pulled them down my legs and off my feet. Firm hands on my thighs, he held me in place while lowering his face to my pussy. Blue eyes on me, he ghosted his tongue up and down my seam. Feather light at first, but quickly growing firmer as he devoured me.

I lay back against the cool of the desk top, the wood a refreshing contrast to my heated skin.

"Oliver," I whispered. I writhed against his mouth, my breath coming in tiny pants and whimpers. He knew exactly what to do with his mouth to push me hard and fast towards the edge.

His response was to work me harder, drawing my clit between his lips and sucking and nipping.

I wanted to make it last, but I never could with him. Not the first time. Being around him had me on edge so much, I was ready to pitch over in a heartbeat.

He drew his face back from me for a few moments, before diving back in, helping me to last for another minute or two before I came hard against his mouth.

My hips lifted off the desk, but his firm fingers held me so his tongue didn't leave my clit until I'd come down from my orgasm.

He finally took his mouth off my hypersensitive nub and straightened up. He undid the front of his pants, letting his erection spring free, thick and ready. Hands back on my hips, he pulled me towards him, sliding me onto his cock.

His eyes half-closed, he groaned with appreciation. "You're absolutely incredible. I forget how good you feel until you're around my dick." He pulled my legs up until I wrapped them around him, my heels pressed against his bare ass.

"I love having you inside me," I whispered. "Don't hold back."

"With you? Never." He thrust inside me like a man who wasn't sure he'd get the chance again. Like he wanted a memory to keep him warm at night. Not just now. Every time we fucked, it felt like he was fully appreciating every centimetre of my pussy. With him, I never felt taken for granted. He made me feel like I was a goddess, him worshipping every bit of my body.

My back slid across the top of the desk, over and over while he pounded into me.

"If I could freeze time, I'd freeze this, right here," he ground out between thrusts. "Being buried inside you is everything. I never want to stop." He rolled his hips, driving himself deeper and deeper. Every stroke was stronger than the last, hitting me all the way through, like he was trying to become a part of me.

"That feels so good," I said breathlessly. "Don't stop."

"I won't." He pressed a hand between us to rub my clit. "Come with me. I want to feel your pussy squeeze my cock."

"I'm so close," I said. "Just a few more…ahhh, there." I came harder than before, taking him with me.

Our groans and moans mingled together so I could hardly tell who was making which sound. It didn't matter. The only thing that did was the rush of blood through my body, the fireworks of bliss in my vision, the way he went still as he spilled himself inside me.

We panted together, both coming down from our high, holding each other as tight as we dared. Skin on skin, warm and comforting, slick with his leaking cum.

Another beautiful, stolen moment neither of us would regret. Another one we'd have to keep a cherished secret from the world.

For now.

CHAPTER 10
TOBY

I leaned to the right, snapping out my glove and letting the puck come to me. Like the catch was nothing, I tossed it back in Easton's direction. The puck slid across the ice to stop at his feet.

"You're on fucking fire today." Cruz grinned at me and stole the puck from Easton before the other winger could move.

I shrugged. "I'm always on fire, bro."

Yeah, we lost the first game, but that was in the past. No more pucks were getting past me for the rest of the season. Okay, maybe one or two, just to make the opposition feel like they weren't complete losers compared to us.

"You weren't on fucking fire on Friday night," Elliott snarled.

"Did you go home to your hand?" Cruz teased.

Elliott growled and started toward Cruz, gloved

hand curled in a fist. He shoved into him, pushing Cruz backwards towards the boards.

"Back the hell off," Kage Foster shouted. "Save the aggression for the opposition."

Cruz held his hands up to either side, stick hanging from his fingers. "Sorry, Coach."

Elliott grumbled under his breath and all but stomped away.

Easton muttered something that sounded suspiciously like, "He's a fucking dickhead," before skating over to the puck and slamming it toward the goal, trying to catch me unaware.

I stopped it with my stick and grinned. "You're gonna have to get up much earlier to take me by surprise."

Easton grinned back. "You can't blame a guy for trying."

"That, I cannot," I agreed. I shook out my arms and legs and fended off another attempted goal, this time by Cole Davies. Motherfucker almost got it past me, but I stopped it right before the puck slid past my left skate.

I sent it spinning back. Before I could blink, he'd flicked it past me and into the back of the net.

"Now that's how you do it." Easton offered him a fist bump.

I grunted my annoyance. I wasn't going to be a bitch about it; it was my fault he got the puck past me. I was quick, but this time he was quicker. I appreciated his skill. We'd need that to win.

"Take a break," Kage shouted.

I nodded and skated over to step off the ice.

"Glover," Elliott said, his eyes narrowed at me.

"Quinn." I barely gave him a glance in return.

"Who was that chick you were with the other night?" He opened a bottle of water and took a swig.

"None of your business." I picked up my own water and had a sip.

"Didn't put out for you either?" He seemed amused, like he'd said something hilarious.

He didn't see my fist coming until I planted it in the middle of his face. He reeled back against the wall, blood pouring from his nose.

"Fucking asshole." He lunged at me, but Cole grabbed him before he could take a swing.

"Do you both want to get benched for the rest of the season?" Cole hissed. He directed the question at me, while still gripping Elliott. His expression strongly suggested I should back down, Elliott wasn't worth it.

"What did I say about saving your aggression for the opposition?" Kage stomped over and glared at all of us. "Quinn, go and have that seen to. As for the rest of you, save your fucking fists for the ice."

"Sorry, Coach." I could apologise for irritating him, but not for what I did to Elliott's face. The prick had it coming. If I hadn't punched him out, someone else would have.

Cole stepped back and let Elliott stomp away. "He's only trying to get a rise out of you."

"I know, but saying shit like that about Marley pisses me off," I said. No one talked smack about her and got away with it. No one talked smack about any woman around me and didn't hear about it. He could save being a dickhead for somewhere else. Guys like him were all fucking talk anyway.

"Me too," Cole said.

I picked up my water bottle and drank down what was left, my eyes on Cole. In just those two words, he caught my interest.

"You know Marley?"

"I've seen her around," he said, momentarily looking uneasy and cagey.

"And?" I prompted. If I had more competition for her, I wanted to know about it.

"And what?" he asked. "She didn't notice me in high school, she's not going to notice me now."

I took a good, long look at him. I won't say I hadn't noticed him before, I absolutely had. I was paying more attention now though. He was a good looking guy, but didn't say much. An excellent hockey player, he kept to himself off the ice, except when he was stopping other guys from being dicks.

"Did you ever try to talk to her?" I asked.

His cheeks actually went pink. "No. Apart from one time when I asked her to pass me something in class. I don't think she even remembers we went to the same school. I was the nerd in the corner."

I grinned. "Ain't nothing wrong with being the nerd.

Not that I was ever one." I was the guy who played every sport he could get his hands on until I found one I really enjoyed. School and I, we didn't get along so well. I only passed because I needed the scholarship to a school with a hockey team good enough for the NHL to scout from.

"Of course you weren't," Cole said. "You would have had your pick of women, while guys like me tried to avoid getting beat up." His gaze flicked towards the floor.

"And here you are now, playing professional hockey," I said. "Fighting off women left and right." Come to think of it, I hadn't seen him with anyone. "Or fighting off men."

I watched carefully for his reaction to that. He was just the kind of guy I was into, if he felt the same way. If not, that was cool. I wasn't everyone's cup of java.

He twitched.

Yeah, that was what I thought.

"There's no shame in being bisexual." I was blunt, but kept my voice down, if only to keep the rest of the team from hearing and being dickheads about it towards him. Although, if they did, I'd happily plant my fist in their face too.

"I know," Cole said quickly. "I've just never been good at relationships with…anyone."

I patted him on the back. "It's never too late to figure out shit like that. Want to get a drink after training?" I've always been one to jump in with both feet and to hell with the consequences. Life, in my assessment, was too short to hold back.

He gaped at me for a few moments in surprise. "I..."

"No pressure," I said.

"I'd like that," he said finally. "Unless it's going to cause a problem with Marley."

"Trust me, she'll be cool with it," I said. I told her I wanted to be with her, but I wouldn't rule out having other guys in this relationship with her. Maybe it would be Cole and maybe it wouldn't. There was no harm in exploring and finding out.

"Great," he said. "I'll look forward to it. But...there's something you should know."

I raised an eyebrow at him. "What's that? Don't tell me you and your twin brother are a package deal, because if you are, I'm out of here." Saxon Davies was way too much of a meathead for me.

Cole grimaced. "No. I was just going to say I'm not going to cut you any slack. On the ice, I mean. If I get an opportunity to get the puck past you, I'm going to take it."

"You fucking better take it," I growled playfully. "I don't want any special treatment from anyone. Not for any reason. If you get that puck past me, it's because you played better than I did."

I pointed a finger roughly in the direction of his nose. "The same goes for you too. I'm never going to step aside and let anyone take a goal, no matter who they are. Something you should know about me, I'm as competitive as shit. I hate losing. All I've ever wanted, all my life, was to be the fucking best."

"Me too," he said softly. His eyes were suddenly glazed, his expression troubled, haunted, like this conversation opened a wound that never healed.

"Did you get beaten up a lot?" I asked. He'd mentioned trying to avoid that. I sensed there was a deeper meaning behind those words. Something both dark and painful. Raw.

He flinched at my direct question. "You could say that."

"Kids from school? Who do I have to beat the snot out of?" I was only half-joking. For some reason, he brought out my protective side. I hated nothing more in this world than a bully.

He glanced down at the ground. "Not from school." He barely spoke above a whisper.

My blood went cold. "Fuck. At home?" That was even worse. Home was the place everyone should feel safe, not bruised or broken.

He looked back up, eyes wide. "I'm supposed to be a big, bad hockey player..."

I put a hand on his shoulder and squeezed, trying to connect through the padding. "I'm guessing you weren't a big, bad hockey player back then. You were just a kid. Anyone who lays a hand on a kid should have their balls ripped off and shoved down their throat."

"Yeah," he said. "He called me a sissy until I started

playing hockey and got bigger than him. But it still sucks, you know?"

"I do know," I said. "You might be surprised how many guys out there grew up like that. People who do it, they're nothing but motherfucking cowards." If I met the guy who did this, I'd do more than punch his lights out.

"Look at you now though," I said. "You're a fucking wall of smoking hot muscle. I'd bet anything you have eyes following you everywhere you go and you just haven't noticed it yet."

His cheeks were adorably pink. "I don't know about that." He really was convinced no one noticed him, wasn't he? There was something endearing about a guy who had no idea how attractive he was.

"I do," I said firmly. "I'm going to prove it to you. We'll have a drink and I'll point out every single person who stopped to stare at you. By the time we're done, your head is going to be bigger than Cruz's. If that's humanly possible."

There was nothing wrong with his healthy ego. Cruz might even be competition for me in that department.

Cole looked like he didn't think that was possible. "About the way I feel about Marley…"

"I'm not threatened by you," I said. "Women like Marley, there's room in her heart for all the love. Hell, I'll even set you up on a date with her. That's how much I'm not threatened."

"You'd do that?" he asked. "What if we— I mean, you and I..."

He looked confused as hell, clearly trying to get his head around all of this. It was a lot, but like always, I saw what I wanted and went after it. If that was too much for him and he wanted to walk away, I'd understand. Sometimes, I was too much for myself.

"I see no reason why we can't both be with her and with each other, if that's what happens," I said.

This was way too soon for me to mention Oliver, especially with all three of Cat's boyfriends standing a handful of metres away. If they overheard, she'd find out about thirty seconds later. That would be bad for everyone concerned. I wanted Marley and Oliver's relationship out in the open as much as they did, but for Cat to find out that way could destroy everything.

"If this is some kind of dream, I don't want to wake up," Cole said. He looked a bit like a little kid at Christmas. I suspected he hadn't had as many good Christmases as he should have. Once again, I was furious at whoever took that away from him. I was tempted to ask who, but that was something he'd tell me when he was ready.

I hoped.

I chuckled. "It's not a dream, I'm just that awesome." I wasn't known for being all that humble. Life was too short for that shit. I preferred to be myself, whatever the consequences. Even if it meant having a sore hand after punching Elliott. It would be a whole lot worse if I wasn't wearing gloves. For him and for me.

"Yeah, you are," Cole agreed. His gaze dropped to my mouth. He swallowed audibly.

So did I. If we weren't in the middle of training, I'd kiss the hell out of him. I might have done it anyway, but the goalie coach called out my name for me to go and train with him.

"Later." I patted his shoulder again before walking back onto the ice.

CHAPTER 11
MARLEY

The atmosphere in O'Reilly's was electric. The Ghouls walked in, followed by a round of cheers. Cruz and Easton both bowed before joining Cat and Shaw in the corner.

Toby did his own wave to the crowd before joining Eden and me at the bar. He draped his arm over my shoulder and kissed my cheek.

"Good game tonight," I said. I nestled into him before Eden made a face and slipped away.

"Something I said?" he drawled.

"She's just giving us some space." I gestured to the bar attendant to make us a round of drinks. He nodded and placed a beer in front of Toby and wine in front of me. I nodded my thanks and tapped my card to pay.

"I appreciate her doing that." Toby picked up his drink and offered me a toast.

"To the first win of the season," I said. They'd scraped through in overtime with a score of five goals to four, but it was still a win.

"The first of many," he said. "We're just warming up around here." He grinned and knocked back half his drink in one go.

"I'll drink to that." I took a smaller sip. I didn't want to get shitfaced. The last time I did, I threw up on someone's shoes. I didn't even know who. I didn't need that kind of embarrassment in my life more than once.

"Cole." Toby gestured him over. "You were on fire tonight." He offered the defenceman a fist bump.

Cole bumped and leaned against the bar beside me. "Hey."

I'd had a bit of a crush on Cole Davies for a long time, but this was the closest I'd ever been to him, as far as I knew. He'd never seemed particularly interested in me.

"Hey," I said. "Toby is right, you played so well. It seemed like you were everywhere. That final goal Cruz got in with your assist, I wouldn't have believed it if I hadn't seen it with my own eyes." They'd moved so fast I barely saw the puck before it was slamming into the net.

"Toby is always right when it comes to hockey," Toby said with a chuckle.

"Does Toby always talk about himself in third person?" I teased. Now I was picturing him naked, telling an enraptured Internet audience about Cole's assist.

"Sometimes," Toby said. "Only when he's especially impressed." He gave Cole a piercing look.

I glanced between them. Cole's cheeks were slightly pink. The vibes they were giving off suggested they were into each other. That would explain why Cole wasn't interested in me. Only...now he was looking at both of us the same way.

His Adam's apple bobbed and he glanced down at the worn hardwood floor. After a few beats, he glanced back. "Just doing my job."

It never occurred to me before that he might just be shy. So many of the guys on the team were outgoing, their personalities so strong they overshadowed the people around them. It was easy to assume they were all like that, but evidently that assumption was wrong.

"You do it well." I put a hand on his bicep. His muscle was rock hard under my palm.

"Thanks," he said awkwardly. "I appreciate that."

"I appreciate the way you stuck up for me the other week," I said. "With Elliott and Saxon. It was...kinda hot."

He looked at my hand resting on his arm. "My brother gets out of hand sometimes. Elliott too. Someone has to keep an eye on them."

"Shouldn't have to be you, bro," Toby said. "You're here to have fun too."

"Yeah." Cole didn't look like he entirely believed

that. "Sometimes it's easier to stop shit before it happens, you know? Those two like to think they can do whatever they want to whoever they want. Sooner or later, they're going to overstep, hard."

"It's not your responsibility to pick up the pieces," Toby said. "They're grown men. You gotta live your life."

"Toby is right again," I said.

"Some kinda record," Toby said jokingly. He downed the rest of his drink and placed his empty glass back on the bar. "Come on, let's dance."

He gestured toward the crowded dance floor in front of the live band that was rocking out to the side of the pub.

Cole looked like he might argue, but Toby grabbed both of our hands and pulled us through the crowds.

We squeezed into a space on the edge of the dance floor. Toby stood in front of me and manoeuvred Cole to stand behind me. Toby grabbed my arms and draped them over his shoulders, pulling me close until my body was pressed against his.

Cole placed his hands on my shoulders, his pelvis lightly touching my ass.

The warmth from both of their bodies penetrated my clothes all the way down, past my skin.

The band started to play a slow song, the guitar a smooth accompaniment to the keyboard and the lead singer's husky vocals. If the guys didn't get me going, the music would.

In near perfect unison, we swayed, bodies grinding against each other. I was quickly breathless.

Holy shit. I'd never been in the middle of a hockey god sandwich, but I liked it. I went on swaying, my ass rubbing against Cole's cock until he was hard. Both of their erections pressed into me. My panties were completely and utterly ruined.

"Maybe we should get out of here." Toby brushed hair off my neck and leaned in to kiss my throat. He lifted his face, looked towards Cole and said, "All of us."

Was he suggesting what I thought he was suggesting? Because if he was, I was here for it.

"If Marley wants to." Cole stroked his thumb across the side of my neck, making me hotter still.

"Marley wants to," I said. "Very much."

"Let's go then." Toby gripped my hand and Cole took the other. Linked like that, we made our way to the door and out into the cool of the night.

"My place isn't far," Toby said.

Cole stopped to glance back at the pub, an uneasy expression on his face again.

"Let your brother deal with his own shit," Toby told him. "Let's go and have some fun." Without waiting for further argument, he led us to a small apartment building a block from the pub.

I admit to doing a quick glance back of my own. Oliver hadn't been at the pub or the game tonight, it was his turn to be on call at the hospital. I missed his presence, if not having to dodge Cat.

I pulled out my phone and sent off a quick text, explaining where I was going and why. I had his blessing, but I wanted him to know exactly what was happening. Going around behind my friends' backs was bad enough without feeling like I was doing anything behind his.

He responded a minute or two later with a text saying,

Have fun. Those boys better give you plenty of orgasms.

I smiled and replied with,

They will.

I hoped.

Both of them pressed close to me, we travelled up the elevator to the third floor. Toby unlocked his door and waved us both inside. The door barely closed behind us before his mouth was on mine, and Cole's hands were sliding up the back of my Ghouls jersey.

"Are you sure we're not going too fast?" I asked. Toby and I had agreed not to, but now, in the heat of the moment, it would be easy to get carried away.

"I'm sure," Toby said between kisses. "If you are?"

"I'm sure," I said. I glanced over my shoulder to Cole.

"As long as you both want me here, then I'm sure too," Cole said. He looked pained, like if we stopped now, he'd have to get himself off in the elevator on the way down to the ground floor.

"We do," I said. Not just because I didn't want him to have to do that.

I turned to face him and pressed my palms to his rock hard chest. I looked him right in the eyes and tangled my fingers in his shirt. I pulled him down so I could kiss his mouth.

He tasted like bourbon and ginger. Masculine and spicy, but sweet at the same time. His lips were the perfect, soft contrast to the rasp of his stubble against my skin.

I tugged up the front of his shirt and pulled it off over his head. He let it drop to the floor.

"Holy shit, you're beautiful," I said. His body was all firm muscle, perfect dips and planes, with scars here and there.

His cheeks went pink. "I don't know about that."

"I do," Toby said. "You're fucking gorgeous. Both of you." He turned me back around to face him and kissed me while helping me out of my jersey.

Cole unhooked my bra and pushed the straps down my arms before cupping my breasts from behind and palming my nipples.

Toby kissed my mouth and down my cheek to my neck before breaking off and pressing his mouth to Cole's.

I leaned my head back slightly to watch them make out with each other. Holy puck that was hot.

Toby slid his tongue across Cole's lower lip and

inside his mouth. He thrust it in and out a few times like he was fucking his mouth.

Cole moved one of his hands from my breast down to Toby's erection, which looked as though it was trying to split the seam of his jeans.

Toby undid his pants and pushed them and his boxers down, letting his cock free. He gently took Cole's hand and wrapped it around his length.

Cole's blush deepened, but he pumped Toby a handful of times before swallowing hard and sinking to his knees. He looked up at Toby and me, then slowly licked the head of Toby's cock.

"Oh, yeah," Toby breathed. "That feels good."

Cole closed his mouth around Toby's tip and started to suck. His lips made a soft, wet sound as his lips worked, sliding back and forth with each bob of his head.

I shimmied out of the rest of my clothes and knelt down beside Cole. I worked his jeans down and curled my fingers around his cock. He was hard as a rock, a thick vein throbbing at the base of his length.

He groaned and thrust into my hand. He pulled his mouth off Toby. His voice husky, he said, "I want to be inside you."

I guided him off Toby and replaced him, the goalie's cock in my mouth while I got on all fours. Cole scooted around behind me, kissed my ass cheek a couple of times before pushing his fingers deep into my pussy.

"You're so wet already." He sounded amazed and surprised.

I hummed my agreement and went on sucking and licking, teasing Toby with my lips and tongue.

Cole slid out his fingers, positioned his cock and thrust into me. With one stroke, he was fully seated inside me. He was still for a while before he started to thrust. He pressed a hand between us, rubbing my clit in time with his movements.

I looked up to see Toby watching us, his lips slightly apart.

"That's fucking hot," he said. "Fuck her harder."

Cole did. Pounding into me with more and more force, grunting each time. His fingers were relentless on my clit, pinching and rolling until all I could do was come, screaming around Toby's cock.

Cole followed a moment later, his hips stilling as he came inside me.

"Just like that." Toby grabbed my hair and pulled my mouth off his cock. He waited until Cole slid out of me before turning me around, kneeling behind me and slamming his cock into my pussy.

He groaned, long and low. "Fucking hell, that's good." He snaked an arm around the back of Cole's neck, pulling him in for a kiss at the same time as he was fucking me.

Between the sensation of him sliding in and out of me, and the wet sound of their kisses, I couldn't stop myself from coming again. And again.

The third time I came, Toby came with me, thrusting frantically before adding his cum to Cole's inside my body. I felt so full I'd probably leak for days, but I loved every minute of it. I'd never been with two smoking hot guys before. The fact they were into each other too added to the heat level by approximately a billion percent.

Toby sagged over me, puffing lightly. "Let's get cleaned up. Then it's time for round two."

CHAPTER 12
MARLEY

"You okay?" I asked softly. I put a hand on Cole's shoulder. He was looking out the window, but his eyes were glazed like he saw nothing.

He startled slightly and turned his face toward me. "Yeah, everything's fine. I just..."

"Regret sleeping with me and Toby?" I spoke as gently as I could. I didn't want him to have regrets, but if he did I wanted to help him deal with them. If he'd let me.

"No," he said quickly. "I was hoping neither of *you* would." His eyes flicked toward Toby, who was in the kitchen making bacon and eggs for breakfast. He'd insisted he didn't need any help, so we left him to it. "I mean, neither of you know me well. People do things in the heat of the moment and then..." He shrugged one shoulder and returned his gaze to the street below.

"I have absolutely no regrets," I said. "I sincerely doubt Toby bothers with them."

He seemed like the kind of guy who lived his life without looking back over his shoulder. He was along for the ride and intended to enjoy every moment of it. "Maybe we can get to know each other? I've always thought you were cute."

He let out a surprised half bark, half laugh. "I don't think I've been called cute for a long time. Not since—"

A heavy silence fell.

"You don't have to tell me, but not since what?" I asked gently. "When?"

He turned around to face me and cupped my cheek with his hand. "Not since I was a kid. My mother used to call me that. But then my father started to laugh at her for doing it. He said she was babying my brother and me. He said we'd end up girly. He wanted us both to be, you know, manly men. My brother did, I guess, but that's not me. I'm not like him."

"Firstly, there's nothing wrong with being girly," I said. "Whether you're a girl, guy or non-binary. Secondly, I've met plenty of manly men." I used air quotes. "They're usually loudmouth assholes." The team had their share of them. Hell, Opal Springs had its share of them.

"Like Saxon," Cole said.

"I wasn't going to name him specifically, but if the rugby jersey fits." I offered an apologetic smile.

"Loudmouth asshole sums him up pretty well," Cole

agreed. He glanced down. "I worry about anyone he gets involved with. He's so much like our father."

I'd dealt with more than enough victims of violence at work to recognise one when he was standing right in front of me.

"It's up to you if you want to talk about it, but I'm guessing your father got rough?" I leaned into his hand and looked up into his brown eyes.

"Yeah, he did," Cole whispered. "I've never told anyone about it until I told Toby. He has that way of making people want to open up to him." His cheeks went pink again. "Figuratively and literally."

My own face heated slightly too. "He definitely does." I swallowed to get my brain back on track. "I'm sorry your father did that to you. You don't deserve that. No one does."

"I used to think I did," Cole said. "He told me I provoked him. Then I got older and realised Saxon got away with worse things than I did. I thought my father hated me, but I got older and realised he was a bully." He ran his thumb up and down my cheek. "I'm sorry, I shouldn't be dumping all of this on you."

"I don't mind at all," I said. "I like that you feel you can open up to me." After a moment I added, "Literally and figuratively."

He chuckled. "I'd open up to you any time. I've been wanting to get to know you for ages."

"Same to you," I said. "I told my friends you have the most grabbable ass I've ever seen. I just thought you weren't interested in me." Or anyone else, that I'd noticed.

"I wasn't good enough." Before I could correct him, he added, "I didn't *feel* good enough."

He continued after a long pause. "If my father was good at anything, it was making me feel like I wasn't as good as everyone else. I've been working on it for a while, but I've been busy with the team. I thought if I was busy enough I wouldn't have to think too much about…anything. Especially when I was working a full-time job and training."

"What were you before you were a professional hockey player?" I asked.

He looked like a guy who was good with his hands. He'd proven that last night, and then some.

He grimaced. "I was a plumber." He closed his eyes and his grimace deepened. "Like my father. There was a time when I thought if I followed in his footsteps, maybe he'd start to give a shit. That probably sounds all kinds of fucked up."

"That sounds perfectly normal to me," I said. "I've done plenty of things in my day to get my parents' attention. We're pretty close, but they wanted me to be more ambitious in life. As if I would have been any good as a doctor or a lawyer." I snorted.

"You give great examinations." His voice was low and husky. "I might need more of them. Just to be safe."

"We wouldn't want you to be unsafe or unwell," I said with a smile. I stood on my toes and pressed my lips to his. Something about kissing him felt comfortable and familiar. As if we'd known each other in a past life or something. He and Toby. I could easily have known them for as long as I'd known Oliver.

And yet, I knew very little about either of them.

"What's your favourite colour?" I asked.

"Orange," he replied. "I know, no one else's favourite colour is orange. I think I chose it because my father hates it so much."

"Secretly a rebel, I like that," I said. "Mine is blue. Star sign?"

"Aries. Saxon is a Taurus. I was born a few minutes before midnight and he was born a few minutes after. Our birthdays are on different days."

"That's cool," I said. "It would be funnier if you were born in different months, or different years."

"Sometimes it feels like we were," he said. "Like I was born five years before him, not five minutes."

"The curse of being the oldest child." I gave him a sympathetic look. "I'm the classic youngest child. Got away with all sorts of things. I have two older brothers who raised hell. I was basically an afterthought."

"I doubt that," Cole said. "No one could ever forget anyone as beautiful as you. But I can imagine what that would have been like. I have two older brothers too. They both left home around the time I started school. Were you close with yours?"

"If by close you mean was I the lookout every time they wanted to get up to shit, then yes," I said. "I was always forgiven because my parents said I was too young to know any better. I totally knew better." I grinned.

"Why do I get the impression you were the one raising hell?" he asked.

"Who, me?" I fluttered my eyelashes. "I'd never put a toe out of line. Much."

He laughed softly. "You didn't tell me your star sign."

"I'm a Scorpio," I said. "Classic, mysterious, sensual and loyal to a fault." All of the things Oliver said he loved about me. That was something I was going to have to explain to Cole. I liked him too much to keep that a secret from him. The question was, could I trust him not to say anything?

He cocked his head at me. "What's on your mind? I can see the thoughts tumbling around."

"Am I that obvious?" I asked. I fucking hoped I wasn't. I couldn't be, or Eden and Cat would already know, and if they did, one or both would have confronted me about it by now. And Cat would have confronted her father.

"I'm good at reading people," Cole said with a shrug. "You don't have to tell me."

"Yes I do," I said. "Because I like you and because you opened up to me. It's the least I can do, but if you want to walk away, I'll understand."

His brow creased. "You eat pizza with egg on it?"

I pretended to gag. "What? Hell no. No offence to

people who do, but yuck. It's nothing like that." I took a deep breath and told him how I was fucking my boss and best friend's father. I told him about Cat and why no one could know, for now.

Cole listened and nodded slowly. "I remember when Cruz and Easton used to talk about her in the locker room. I wanted to punch them both in the face." He looked like maybe she was crazy for forgiving them, but that was up to her. "I won't tell anyone. Kids deserve the best start in life, including having mothers who don't lose their mind over what their fathers are doing."

"You think it's wrong?" I asked.

"Let me ask you this." He moved his hand from my cheek to my shoulder. "Do you think your relationship is based on what power he has over you as your boss and an older guy?"

I thought about that for a moment. "This might seem really fucked up, but yes. That's what I like about it. I like it when he takes control. With him, I can let go."

"Can you say no?" he asked.

"Yes, but I don't want to," I said. "I want him to use my body however he wants to. I get off on it."

Cole swallowed. "So if I wanted to—"

My whole body was suddenly trembling with need. Throbbing and aching to be touched. "I'd do it. What-ever it is."

He hesitated for a moment before he grabbed my hair and turned me around. He pushed me to the back of the couch and bent me over it. His hands were on my pants, undoing the button before pulling them and my panties down.

"Are you sure?" he asked, his voice breathless.

"Yes. Yes." I kicked off my pants and stuck out my ass.

He worked his pants down just far enough to free his erection. One hand in my hair, he guided his cock to my entrance and slammed right into me from behind.

I cried out in a combination of pleasure and pain, slightly taken aback the conversation had taken such an abrupt turn. At the same time, loving every moment of it.

He pounded into me over and over, harder and harder, his fingers gripping my hips so hard they'd leave bruises later.

I was vaguely aware of Toby stepping out of the kitchen and coming over to watch us as Cole fucked me relentlessly.

I closed my eyes as a surge of pleasure grew so fast it threatened to overwhelm me. "I'm going to come."

"Do it," Cole ordered.

I tried to hold back, but I couldn't. My orgasm washed over me in a rush. My vision went black and all that was left was his cock thrusting hard enough to wreck my pussy, and the feeling of pure bliss.

Cole followed a moment later, falling still as he came inside me, spilling hot cum into my body.

He sagged over me, trying to catch his breath before sliding out of me and letting go of my hair.

"Fucking hell." He staggered back, pulling his pants back up. "I'm so sorry. I shouldn't have—"

I straightened up. "It's okay. I told you I wanted you to. I liked it. Every minute of it."

He shook his head. "I've never been rough like that."

Bare from the waist down, I stepped towards him, hand out like he was a wild animal. His cum trickled down the inside of my leg.

"I promise you, I liked it," I said. "I like you. I want you to fuck me like that again. When you're ready." This was clearly not a side of himself he'd let loose before. I hoped he'd let it loose again.

He looked stricken. "I'm always so careful. I don't... I don't hurt my partners."

"If you never want to do that again, I'll understand," I said. "But if you do, I'm here for it. You don't always have to be in control. Sometimes it's okay to let go and let the other person be in control." When he looked confused I added, "If I asked you to stop, you would have. Wouldn't you?"

"Of course," he said quickly. He glanced at Toby like maybe the other player should have stopped him.

"Marley was in control the whole time," Toby said. "She was the one calling the shots and letting you fuck her like that. All you did was let go and let your body guide you. It's good to let go a little. Or a lot. This is a safe space, the three of us. If you want to explore all sides of yourself, you can. If you ask me, I think it's healthy to be rough in positive ways. Like a good, hard fuck. Ain't no harm in it. Now, who wants breakfast?"

"I do." I offered my hand to Cole, hoping he'd take it. I understood his reservations, but he was not his father. If I could, I'd help him to understand that.

CHAPTER 13
COLE

I wanted to punch myself in the face. If my father was here right now, I'd let him do it. I'd stand still and let him punch the crap out of me.

I heard Marley's words that she enjoyed what we did, but I still hated myself. I let go. I had no control over myself and my actions and I loved every minute of it.

What the fuck was wrong with me that I wanted to do that to her?

Why didn't she hate me as much as I hated myself? Why didn't Toby?

Fuck.

I would have stopped if she told me to, wouldn't I?

Fuck

I flopped down on a bench to the side of the park and scrubbed a hand over my face.

A few uncomfortable truths went through my screwed up mind.

Mostly, I wasn't sure if I could have stopped. Letting go felt so fucking good. Usually, I was in complete control of myself. The only place I let out some of my rage was on the ice. Even there, I hold back.

When I fucked Marley, I hadn't held back anything. What did that say about me? I'd tried to leave my childhood behind, not be like my father. Was I fooling myself? Maybe I was as big an asshole as he was.

"Hey." Kage Foster slowed to a walk and wiped a hand over his brow.

We must both have had the idea of going out for an early run.

"Hey, Coach." I gave him a short nod and hoped like hell he'd keep on jogging.

"You okay, Davies?" He stopped on the footpath a couple of metres away and stood, scrutinising me.

"Yeah. Kinda. I guess." I shrugged. "Nothing I can't deal with."

He regarded me for a moment but didn't move on. Instead, he sat down beside me and adjusted the Velcro on his running shoes.

"I like to think we're a team off the ice as well as on," he started. He glanced over at me sideways. "If anything is troubling you, I'm a good listener. Anything you say stays on this bench."

"I appreciate that," I said. There was no way I would or could tell him everything. What could he do anyway? I was already seeing a therapist. I should give them a call and see if they were available in the next day or two.

Was there any point though? I couldn't tell them everything either.

Kage sat back. "If you don't mind me saying, you always seem like you have something on your mind. All of us have shit we carry around with us. It's up to you if you want to offload some of it. If you don't, that's cool too." He clearly expected me to say something.

"There's a lot of expectations on us," I said slowly. "Sometimes it's difficult to be the person other people expect me to be."

"Other people expect it, or you do?" he asked.

I looked over to where a couple of kids played on the play equipment, laughing and running around. Totally carefree and happy.

"Me, I guess," I said. "I have this image in my head of who I think I should be, but… I dunno. Maybe I can't be that guy."

"Maybe you already are that guy and you're being too hard on yourself," Kage suggested.

I shook my head. "I don't think that guy exists. Maybe he's something I tried to reach for but I'll never get there."

Cool, calm and collected Cole Davies, the total opposite of his father. Instead, I was just like him.

"A wise woman once said that being aware of our shortcomings was the first step to putting them behind us and becoming better people," Kage said. "That wise woman being my mother."

"We can't always put things behind us," I said. "Some things. They're just what they are. Things we can't change, like our eye colour."

"I don't believe there's anything we can't change if we really want to," Kage said.

"What if we don't want to?" I asked, my voice low. I liked the way it felt to do what I did to Marley. I wanted to do it again. If she was here, I'd force her onto her knees and make her suck my cock. My balls ached thinking about it.

"That's a decision only you can make," Kage said. "At the end of the day, you have to live with your choices. Figure out what you can live with and if you're prepared for the consequences of that. If you are, then you have your answer. No one can make you into something you're not. Not even you."

I placed my elbows on my thighs and rested my face on my hands. "That was what I figured."

What were the consequences? Marley said she wanted to do it again. Toby said he was right behind me. Would he let me use him the way she did? If I kept thinking like that, my cock was going to be harder than iron.

If I was honest with myself, I struggled with how I saw myself after what I did. If they didn't judge me, maybe I shouldn't judge myself. I hadn't hit her. I didn't want to. I just wanted to let go for a little while, to stop being so fucking uptight and wound up. If they didn't see anything wrong with that, maybe it was okay.

I needed to talk to them and work out some boundaries. That way, I might find a compromise between violence and control. A balance between the two.

"You look like you've come to some conclusions," Kage said.

"I have. Thanks, Coach." The conflict in my mind wasn't completely stilled, but things were a little clearer now.

He clapped me on the shoulder. "Any time, Davies. You're a good guy, don't forget that. And a fucking good hockey player. One of the best I've seen." He used to play professionally in Canada. If he said that, maybe it was true. He knew his shit.

"Thanks." My face heated. I wished I could find a way to get the blushing under control. Apparently women found it adorable, but it annoyed the hell out of me. I didn't want to be adorable. I wanted to claim the title of big, bad hockey god. The other guys on the team didn't struggle with doing that, why should I?

"You're welcome." He placed his hands to either side of him on the bench and pushed himself to his feet. "I'm gonna keep running before I get too cold."

"Yeah, me too." I stood as well and glanced at my watch. I had another hour before I was supposed to meet Marley and Toby for brunch. Apparently she wanted to introduce me to Oliver. This would be interesting, to say the least.

I stepped into the restaurant and inhaled the smell of coffee. The second thing I noticed was Marley, who sat in a booth in the corner, on her phone. I watched her for a minute or two before slipping into the seat beside her.

She looked up at me and smiled, making my heart do a triple somersault. It did another one when she leaned over and pressed her lips against mine.

"You look good," she told me.

"You look better." I ordered a coffee when the server stopped by the table, and waited until he left before broaching the subject.

"About the other day," I started.

She put down her phone and placed her hand over mine. "I meant what I said about enjoying it. In fact, I was thinking about taking it further, if you wanted to."

Fuck yeah I did.

"You're really not angry at me?" I asked tentatively. "I thought maybe when you'd had time to think about it…"

"I haven't changed my mind about any of it," she said. "I promise I'm not angry at you at all. The exact opposite." Her tongue swiped over her lips. "I could easily fall for you."

My eyes wanted to pop out of my head. My heart raced like crazy, my palms were slick. All from six words.

"I've already fallen for you," I admitted. "I did a long time ago. I wish I'd spoken to you sooner."

"The time wasn't right then," she said with a twitch of her shoulder. "Now it is." She glanced over to the doorway. "Here's Toby and Oliver."

I recognised the older man from team physicals before we turned professional. Now we had our own doctor and physical therapist, but he was often at games with his daughter and her boyfriends.

I stood and shook both of their hands before sitting back down.

Toby slid in beside Marley, Oliver beside him. Toby kissed Marley.

Oliver looked like he wanted to. "My daughter is at work, but I don't know who else might be around," he said. "Having brunch with the three of you might be hard enough to explain without PDA."

"We'll do all the public displays of affection for you, bro," Toby said.

"Thanks," Oliver said dryly. He gave me a nod. "Cole, you're one of us now."

I returned his nod. "So it would seem. Is that a problem?"

"No. Not at all. We all want the same thing. Marley's happiness." The long, lingering look he gave her spoke clearly about his affection for her. He was as head over heels for her as Toby and I were.

"If you gentlemen will excuse me, I need to go to the ladies," Marley said.

I stood to let her out of the booth and sat back down.

"I was hoping to talk to both of you," Oliver said. He looked at us intently, furtive. "Are you both all in with her?"

"Far as I'm concerned, I'm as all in as a guy can be," Toby said.

"Me too," I said. I sensed this was going somewhere and I wasn't sure I'd like what I was about to hear. If I was him, I'd at least consider telling us both to fuck off. He'd have no luck there. I had no plans to fuck off out of her life now. I'd fight him for her if I had to.

"Good, because I've noticed the way Marley looks at my daughter and her belly," Oliver said. "The way she talks about babies." He sat back and let us come to our own conclusions.

I mulled it over for a minute or two. "You think she wants one?"

I hadn't thought that far ahead. Now I did, how did I feel about it? My father was a shitty role model. What if I was just as bad a parent as he was? Worse. No kid deserves to go through what I went through.

"You're not your father," Toby said bluntly. "No way you'd do the things he did."

Oliver's eyebrows rose for a moment, but he absorbed Toby's words without comment or judgement.

"I have no intention of being like him," I said.

"In answer to your question, yes," Oliver said. "I think she does, and we can be the ones to give that to her."

"She's on birth control," Toby said.

"I can deal with that," Oliver said. "All we need to do is keep doing what you're doing. Fuck her. Cum inside her. I'm sure between the three of us, we can give her what she needs."

"Are we going to ask her?" Toby asked.

"Do we need to?" Oliver shrugged. "We know what she wants and needs. As far as I'm concerned, it's our job to make sure she gets that. A child will tie her to all three of us. She already belongs to us, this will just cement that."

I swallowed. Should I have found the idea of getting her pregnant without her clear consent appealing? Probably not, but I did. I wanted to be the one to put my baby inside her. From the look on Toby's face, he wanted to be him. Oliver too, obviously, since it was his idea. Apparently two adult daughters wasn't enough.

"I'm in," I said softly.

"Me too," Toby said. "Let's go ahead and make our woman's dreams come true. Even if she doesn't know they're her dreams yet."

"Good." Oliver sat back. "Between the three of us, we'll give her everything she needs." A small smile crept onto his face. "I can't wait to see her belly start to swell with our child."

Neither could I. My cock was already ready.

CHAPTER 14

MARLEY

"You seemed to get along with Toby and Cole." I glanced up from my computer screen as Oliver stepped out of his treatment room.

"They seem like good guys who genuinely care about you," he said. "If they weren't, I would have chased them both away while you were in the ladies room." He walked over to my desk and gave me a boyish grin that made my heart flip, like it always did.

"I would have liked to see you try," I said. "Together they'd give you a run for your money."

"Together, they would," he agreed. "Separately, not so much." He tossed a cardboard packet onto the desk. "I figured I'd pick these up for you while I was getting some other things."

I glanced down to see the brand of my birth control pills. "That's sweet of you." I scooped them up and dropped them into my bag.

"That's me, sweet." He smiled. "Although, I don't remember being called that before."

I stood up and moved around the desk to stand in front of him. "You're very sweet. You always put the needs of everyone else before your own. I don't think you have a selfish bone in your body." I slid my arms around his neck and softly kissed his mouth.

"This is selfish," he said, kissing me back. "If I wasn't selfish, I would never have laid a hand on you."

"I thought you did it to make me happy," I said, half teasing.

He looked me in the eyes and smiled. "When you put it that way, maybe you're right. I'm as selfless as they come." He made a face, clearly poking fun at himself.

"I think you are." I kissed him again before stepping back.

Lucky I did, because the door opened a handful of moments later and Eden walked inside. In her hand she held a huge bunch of flowers.

"These are for you. I figured I'd deliver them direct-ly." Her florist shop was in the building beside this one. We met when I went in there one day to buy some fresh flowers for the surgery.

"They're beautiful." I took them from her and looked at the card.

Hey beautiful, can't wait for dinner tonight. Love, Toby

"That's so sweet," I said. I glanced at Oliver, who seemed unsurprised and pleased at the gesture.

"Very sweet." He gave me a secretive smile before heading back into his treatment room.

"So, things are going well with Toby," Eden said. She leaned her hip against my desk. "And Cole?"

"I like both of them and they both like me," I said. I hurried over to the sink in the surgery's kitchenette and filled a vase with water to put the flowers in. I placed the vase on the corner of my desk.

"How do you feel about dating two guys at once?" Eden asked.

I desperately wanted to tell her there were three, but I didn't. Instead I said, "I can already tell communication is going to be really important, from all sides. Lucky for me, I like to talk."

I walked back to the kitchenette and turned on the kettle.

Eden laughed. "I've noticed that about you."

I grabbed three mugs and spooned in coffee and sugar. "What can I say, I've never been shy."

"That's one of the things I like the most about you," she said. "You don't mind saying what you're thinking. There's no pretense like there is with so many other people. You're honest and loyal. I adore that about you."

"Yeah, loyal like a Scorpio," I said.

And lying through my teeth about my relationship with Oliver. I was starting to wonder if there was any way I could possibly tell her and Cat without losing both of them. And Oliver too, if Cat forced him to pick a side. I could lose everything.

Was wanting to be with him selfish? Could I let him go to stop my world from imploding?

I didn't want to. I couldn't imagine the rest of my life without him in it. Thinking about it made my heart hurt.

I pushed my glasses back up my nose and poured hot water into the mugs. I gave them all a stir and handed one to Eden.

"Excuse me for a moment." I took another coffee over to Oliver's treatment room and tapped on the door before stepping inside and placing his on his desk.

He was talking to someone on the phone, so he nodded his thanks and turned his attention back to his call.

I gave him a long look before slipping out of the office and closing the door behind me.

"He's lucky to have you, you know," Eden said. She tucked a strand of purple hair behind her ear.

I gaped at her for a moment before realising she meant he was lucky to have me as an employee.

"Right." I cleared my throat. "Yes. Yes, he is. Lucky for him, he knows it too. Who else would bring him coffee?" Or choke on his cock several times a week?

"You do a lot more than bring him coffee," she said with a laugh. "I'm sure he'd be lost without you. You know what they say about good staff being hard to find."

"I'm sure he'd find another office manager to replace me if he had to," I said. "Tons of people can do what I do." Not *exactly* what I did. I shouldn't like the idea that he'd be lost without me as much as I did, but here we were.

"But how many can do it by looking as good as you do?" she asked.

I glanced down at my sage green blouse, black pencil skirt and kitten heels. "Probably tons, but thanks for the vote of confidence. I adore how supportive you always are."

She put down her coffee and gave me a hug. "What are friends for? To share all our secrets and lift each other up."

Once again, I itched to tell her what was going on. If it wasn't for Cat's pregnancy, I would have spilled everything then and there.

"What is it?" Eden asked. "You keep getting this look on your face like… I don't know. Something is troubling you. You know you can tell me anything, right?"

Anything but this.

I forced a smile. "I know. Everything is fine. I'm a little overwhelmed with the whole Toby and Cole thing. I mean, I've been admiring Cole's ass for the longest time, and now here we are. It doesn't feel quite real, you know?"

"I was wondering how long it would take one of you to make a move," Eden said. "I saw him looking at you plenty of times. It's about time you got together. And Toby, he seems nice."

"He is nice," I agreed. "They both are."

I couldn't get the memory of Cole bending me over the couch, his hand in my hair, ramming into me like that, out of my head. I couldn't wait for round two. Him taking what he wanted like that, it was hotter than hell. It was one of my fantasies brought to life. Surrendering control to him, while knowing I could tap out at any time, was amazing.

"I'm happy for you," Eden said. "I hope you get your happily ever after, just like Cat. Maybe with lots of babies too."

I smiled softly. "I'm not ready for babies yet, but some day." Not until things with Oliver were sorted out. Not to mention I wanted to get to know Cole and Toby better. There was plenty of time later for that conversation.

"You'll be an amazing mother," Eden said. "I'm looking forward to having babies to play with and then hand back."

I snorted. "You sound like my mother." I mimicked her voice. "*The best thing about being a grandmother is that you can fill them full of sugar and hand them back to their parents.*" I rolled my eyes and laughed. "She's going to be the absolute worst."

"Isn't that what grandparents are for?" Eden asked. "To be the worst, but the best at the same time."

I thought for a moment about Cole's father. There was no way in the world he was going anywhere near any child of mine, grandfather or not. I doubted Cole would want him anywhere near us either. Fortunately, any child I had in the future would have plenty of other grandparents to spend time with. Especially if all three guys were involved. There would be no lack of love in their life.

"That sounds about right," I agreed. "I'm sure Oliver will spoil Cat's baby as rotten as their dads will. That little one is going to have everyone wrapped around their little finger."

"Especially Oliver," Eden agreed. "He seems like the doting grandfather type. Although, being a doctor, he'll probably worry about them just as much." Her eyes widened slightly.

"That sounds accurate," I said. "He certainly fusses over Cat until she's ready to climb the walls." When she was training for the Olympics, he was her coach as well as her father and doctor. It was basically his job to fuss over her. One he clearly enjoyed doing.

"Who fusses over Cat?" Oliver stepped out of his treatment room, empty coffee mug in his hand.

"All of her boyfriends," I said. I gave him a smile so he knew we definitely were talking about him. Of course, we'd never say anything bad about him. I wouldn't, anyway. He was, after all, my boss.

He responded with a grunt-laugh. "That sounds about right. Cat never did like being the centre of that kind of attention. She's always been very independent. She has her hands full with those three boys."

"And now Marley is following in her footsteps," Eden said. She grinned at me. "Now you need a third guy."

I almost choked on my last mouthful of coffee. I coughed a couple of times before I caught my breath.

Oliver lightly patted me on the back before stepping away to put his mug in the sink. It was just the length of contact anyone would expect of a boss and his employee. Not a moment more or less.

"Right. A third guy. I'll think about that." I forced myself to look anywhere but at Oliver. If I did, I was sure Eden would see and immediately understand why. Honestly, she was so perceptive, I wasn't sure how she hadn't noticed before. I could only assume we were better actors than we thought we were, or maybe it never occurred to her something might happen between us. If that was the case, she wouldn't have thought to look for it.

"Maybe you could get a cat instead?" Oliver suggested. "Lucifer is very good company for me now I'm living all alone."

Now I looked over at him. "Of course she is." Lucifer was very sweet, nothing like her name. According to

Cat, her younger sister, Bree, named the cat, and didn't care that Lucifer was female. She'd insisted and the name stuck.

I hated to think of Oliver at home alone on the nights I couldn't stick around, with no one to talk to but a cat. I wanted to stay with him every night. I wanted to wake up every morning beside him.

I forced myself to look away. I hoped like hell everything wasn't just about to blow up in our faces.

CHAPTER 15

MARLEY

"Don't you get enough of this place, being here every day?" I asked.

Toby turned off the engine and twisted around in his seat to grin at me. "I never get tired of this place. The day I do, I might as well give up playing hockey. And that ain't gonna happen anytime soon."

He hopped out of the car and walked around to open my door.

I stepped out and looked over to the ice hockey arena.

In contrast to every other time I'd been here, it was quiet, free of crowds. The car park was empty apart from a couple of other vehicles. A handful of lights were on inside, but it wasn't lit up everywhere like usual.

"Are we allowed in there when no one else is around?" I asked.

He draped his arm over my shoulders and led me towards a side door. "Would I bring you here if we weren't?"

"Probably," I said. "You don't seem like the kind of guy who lets a simple thing like a rule get in your way."

His body rumbled against me as he laughed. "Yeah, well, I've been known to bend a rule or two in my time. For a good cause."

"Only for a good cause?" I teased.

"One hundred percent." He pulled a card out of his back pocket and waved it in front of the scanner beside the door. The light on the handle turned green.

He pushed the door open. "Ladies first."

"Thank you, kind sir." I stepped inside.

He took my hand before the door closed behind us and guided me down a corridor and out to the rink. The surrounding stands were in near darkness, but the ice was illuminated by a couple of big overhead lights. It looked otherworldly somehow, glowing, sparkling white.

"Can you skate?" he asked. He gestured toward two pairs of skates that lay on the ground beside the front row of seats.

"In theory," I said. "I mean, I have in the past, but that was a long time ago. Cat and I used to skate together until she decided to take it seriously. I didn't want to get in her way, you know?"

"Seems to me you've spent a lot of time not wanting

to get in her way." He pressed me down into a chair and pulled off my shoes before starting to put on my skates.

"That's what friends do," I said. "We look out for each other."

"What has she done to look out for you?" He pushed a skate onto my foot and started to lace it up.

"She—" I stopped to think. "She's always there for me when I need to talk."

I couldn't remember the last time we sat down and had a meaningful conversation. At least, not one that involved any other topic than her boyfriends. She confided in me and Eden a lot when they were still being assholes to her. I hadn't shared any of my problems with her, not recently. I didn't want to dump anything on her when she was going through so much.

"Seems to me that goes one way." He double checked the laces before pushing the other skate onto my other foot.

"She had a hard year," I argued lamely.

"People go through shit all the time. Doesn't mean they gotta make it all about themselves." He tied a neat knot and sat beside me to put on his skates.

"She doesn't try to make it about herself," I said. "Maybe it's me. I haven't had anything really big go on in my life recently."

"Nothing you can share, because if you tell her the truth, she might break like some fragile doll," Toby said.

I bristled at that. "You know how complicated that is."

"I know how it doesn't have to be complicated," he said. "If she's the friend you say she is, she'll be cool with whatever you're doing and whoever you're doing it with."

"Are you insisting I tell her?" I didn't like the direction this conversation was taking. "Because you know I can't do that, not yet. If anything happened to her and her baby—"

"I'm not insisting on anything," Toby said. "I just happen to think friendships go two ways. All relationships, matter-of-fact. Open communication is the key to all happiness, or some shit. If there's ever anything you need to tell me, don't hesitate. Don't think it'll piss me off. There's nothing you can say that would make me turn my back on you. Unless you tell me I have to eat my burgers with beetroot from now on." He looked disgusted.

I laughed. "I would never insist anyone eat something they don't want to. Life is too short for that."

"That's why I prefer to eat what I want to." He pushed himself to his feet and crouched down in front of me. He placed his hands on my thighs and rubbed his thumbs up and down the insides. "Like you."

A full body shiver went through me. My clit throbbed in response to his touch. "Should we skate first?"

He grinned. "I love that that's your response. Not that we're in a public place and I shouldn't feast on you." He ran the tip of his tongue over his bottom lip. "I'm tempted to skip right to dessert."

Just when I thought he might, he took my hand and helped me to my feet. He didn't let go while we walked onto the ice. He faced me, held both my hands and started to skate backward, drawing me along with him.

After a few tentative moments, I started to move my feet, just like I had all those years ago. Gradually, he loosened his grip, until finally he let go of one hand and we skated side-by-side, hand in hand.

"And you said you couldn't skate," he teased.

"I didn't say I couldn't, I said it's been a while," I said.

To my surprise, it felt like I hadn't stopped. Everything came back to me with ease. I wasn't ready to take up ice hockey or figure skating, but I could skate around the rink with my boyfriend. Was he that? He made it clear he wasn't walking away from me anytime soon, but that was all. I reminded myself I hardly knew him. There was plenty of time to figure things out. It didn't have to be today.

"You look like you were born to skate," he said. "Maybe you shouldn't have stopped so you could save your friend's feelings. When was the last time you put yourself first for anything?"

"I—" I thought about that for a minute or two. "Every time I'm with Oliver. If I wasn't selfish, I'd give him up. But I haven't. I don't want to."

"But you will if your friend insists on it," he said.

"You'll walk away from him and break your own heart if she says so."

"It wouldn't be fair to come between her and her father," I said.

"Is it fair to come between him and you?" Toby asked. "You know what they say, the heart wants what the heart wants. You really gonna ignore what your heart wants because of someone else? I can't see how anyone wins then. Not you. Not him. Not even her."

"You won't have to share me with him," I pointed out.

He frowned. "You think I care about that? I don't. You know why? Because I care about you. Your happiness. Your satisfaction in every way that counts. For that, I put my own ego aside. Let me tell you, that's no easy feat. My ego is pretty fucking healthy." He grinned.

"I've noticed," I said with a laugh. "I don't think any of this is as simple as you're making it out to be. It's not just me either. Oliver doesn't want to be estranged from his daughter. Or his grandchild. I have to think about him too. What this might do to his relationship with her."

"Was he thinking any of that when he got his dick wet in your glorious pussy?" Toby asked. "He must have known the consequences right from the start. His daughter's best friend. None of that stopped him."

"It didn't stop me either," I said. Maybe it should have. I should have thought about what might happen before I was on my knees, my mouth around his cock.

This was a mess we both created. We'd have to deal with what came out of it.

"It's different for you," Toby said. He squeezed my hand while we skated slow circles around the ice. "He's older and your boss. He had all the power. What would have happened if you said no?"

"I didn't want to say no," I said.

"But if you had," he pressed. "You would have had to look for a different job. He may not have fired you, but things would have been as awkward as fuck. You know it as well as I do."

"I guess so," I said reluctantly. "But that wasn't what happened." After a moment I added, "Should I worry about getting involved with you? You're a famous hockey player. Some would say that gives you power."

He glanced over and grinned. "I guess they might. You and me though, we know better. When it comes to me, and to Cole, you know how to stand up to us. You wouldn't hesitate to kick us in the nuts."

"Don't give me a reason to," I said.

"I wouldn't dream of it." He let go of my hand and turned around, skating backward right in front of me.

"Now you're just showing off," I said. If I tried that, I'd run into the boards.

He spread his arms out to either side. "What's the point of having mad skills if you can't show them off once in a while?"

"Don't you do that every time you step out on the

ice? Surrounded by an arena of adoring fans?" I raised my eyebrows at him.

"Naw, that's work. This is different." He skated in a tight circle before coming back to skate in front of me again.

"Looks like showing off to me," I said.

"What can I say? I've been practising this for a long time. It feels a bit like walking down the street would be showing off my walking skills, or something like that." He shrugged.

"I guess so," I agreed. "Like me typing would be showing off, when it's just work. But your skills look better than mine."

"Mine might be more entertaining to some, but yours help save lives," he said. "We're both awesome, just in different ways."

He skated around to take my hand so we could skate together again. "So you know, this isn't the only thing I brought you here for. I have something else in mind, but I can't get the idea of eating you out of my brain." He guided me over to the side of the rink and turned me until my back was pressed against the boards.

The look he gave me made my heart race. His eyes were dark, growing darker by the moment.

I swallowed. "Here?"

He waved a hand around behind his shoulder. "There's no one else here but us. Except maybe a couple of cleaners. But they have no reason to come here. You, on the other hand, have plenty of reasons to come." He grazed his lips over mine, before claiming my mouth more firmly, more desperate. Like he wanted to eat me alive.

My arms went around his neck. I kissed him back, a clash of teeth and tongues and lips.

He slid his hands up the front of my blue, mohair jumper and white blouse, pinched my nipples through the lace of my bra.

I shivered.

"Cold?" he asked.

"No, that's just what you do to me." I pressed my palm to his firm stomach before sliding it down to the front of his pants. I cupped his groin, feeling his erection grow under my hand.

"That's what you do to me," he said with a chuckle. He pressed himself into my hand a few times before taking hold of the top of my leggings and pushing them and my panties down far enough for him to slide his hand between my legs. Eyes on mine, he teased my clit with his fingertips, grazing over my sensitive skin before sliding a finger inside my wet heat.

"I can't get over the way you feel," he said. "You're always so wet and ready."

He thrust his fingers into me a couple of times, then pulled them out and sank to his knees. He gently pushed my thighs apart and licked all the way up my seam with the tip of his tongue.

"You taste so good," he said. "So fucking good."

I pressed my palms to the boards behind me, supporting myself so I could open my legs wider. Right now, I didn't care if the whole team appeared to watch. The only thing that mattered was the way he was devouring my pussy.

He pushed his fingers back inside me as he licked and nibbled my clit.

"Just like that," I said breathlessly. "That feels perfect." The right spot, the right pressure had my orgasm building slowly, but steadily, more and more blood pooling in my core, throbbing and hot.

He went on working me, a little faster and a little deeper, always watching for my response to even the smallest adjustment. When I thought it was exactly perfect, he showed me it could be even better. Who was this guy who knew my body better than I did?

"Toby," I whispered. "I'm going to come."

Without stopping what he was doing, he nodded, his eyes approving.

Keeping my eyes open, I focused on him while my blood pounded harder. Muscles clenched and a wave of bliss washed me away. I ground myself against him, drawing out every spark, every firework that passed through me, right until I came back down.

His mouth shining, Toby stood, not even slightly awkward on his skates. He pushed my leggings down to my ankles and undid his own pants.

"That's refreshing," he said when the cold air connected with his thick, heated cock.

He turned me around and waited until I grabbed hold of the top of the boards and stuck out my ass. His hands gripping my hips, he guided himself to the entrance of my pussy and pressed inside.

"Ever since I met you, I wanted to fuck you right here, on the ice," he said. "I'm going to fill you up." He pushed in further.

"Yes, please," I said breathlessly. I should have been cold, but his touch kept me warm. That and the way my blood rose again.

"Yes please, what?" he asked.

"I want you to fill me up," I said. "I want you to come inside me."

"That's exactly what I'm gonna do." He pushed himself the rest of the way in and was still for a few heartbeats before he started to thrust into me. "I'm going to fill you more than you've ever been filled before."

I groaned. "Do it. I want every drop."

"It's all yours, baby." He pounded harder, with firm, even strokes. "Every little bit."

The tips of his fingers pressed into my skin, holding me hard while he slid his cock in and out of my body. "Come with me."

I held onto the boards hard to keep from sliding away while I came again, harder than the first time. I shattered into a thousand pieces before slowly coming back together again.

Toby was right behind me, grinding into me and

moaning with his release as he spilled his hot cum into me. "Fuck, yeah. Marley, you're absolute perfection."

My legs were as wobbly as jelly, but I managed to stay upright as he slid out of me and pulled my panties and leggings back into place.

"Let's get you cleaned up," he said. "Then I can fill you up again."

CHAPTER 16
MARLEY

"So this is what you like to do for fun?" I asked.

Toby led me to a large room near the rink, where a blanket was spread out on the carpeted floor. Cushions were piled here and there, along with a bottle of wine, two glasses and three large pizza boxes.

"I didn't know what toppings you liked," he said. "They're all half and half so there's plenty to choose from." He guided me down to the blanket so my back was leaning against one of the piles of cushions.

He sat beside me and frowned. "You do like pizza, right?" He smacked himself in the forehead. "It didn't cross my mind you might not. I can get something else in." He pressed the heel of his hand against the floor, ready to push himself back to his feet.

I caught his wrist. "I love pizza. What's not to love? Bread, melted cheese and a variety of toppings. It's basically the perfect meal."

He relaxed back against the cushions and reached for the bottle and glasses to pour us both wine.

"See, that's exactly how I feel about it. Burgers too. They're basically all the food groups rolled into one. Do me a favour and don't tell Coach I was eating pizza."

"My lips are sealed." I took the glass he offered me and took a sip. "Mmmm. That's so good."

"I have to give it to you Aussies, you know how to make wine." He set down his glass and picked up a remote control to turn on a huge screen on the wall. "We usually watch replays and shit on this. I figured we could put it to better use."

"Should we be doing this here?" I asked. "I mean, what if Kage turns up and busts us eating pizza and drinking wine at your workplace?"

Toby shrugged. "I doubt he's going to turn up here on a Tuesday night. If he does, I'll deal with him." He pressed a couple of buttons before a movie filled the massive screen.

"I wouldn't have thought you'd be a romantic comedy guy," I remarked.

"Don't go telling anyone, but I like me a good romcom." He gave me a nod before putting the remote down and reaching for a box of pizza. He took a slice and passed me the box.

I took one for myself and nestled back against the cushions to eat and watch. "How did you know this was one of my favourites?"

Without looking at me he said, "Lucky guess. You

struck me as the romantic type. The kind who can stand up for herself, but doesn't mind it when the guy does it sometimes. This guy," he nodded towards the screen, "he's got it sorted out. Sure, he makes some mistakes along the way. Who doesn't? But in the end, he's got his shit together."

"Are you trying to say I should end it with Oliver and just go out with you because you've got your shit together?" I asked.

He glanced over and barked a laugh. "I don't know what I did to give you the impression I had anything together, but thanks. I'll take the compliment. For your information, I wouldn't tell you to end anything with anyone. That's the choice you gotta make. Personally, I like Oliver. I am going to punch his lights out if he hurts you though. Same with Cole." He settled back against the cushions again.

"All I'm saying is that you're worth it," he said. "I'm going to do my best to get my shit together, for you. Before..."

I frowned. "Before what?"

He cleared his throat. "Before you realise I'm a hot mess and end it with me instead."

I didn't think that was what he was going to say, but his lips were pressed together in a tight line, like he wasn't going to elaborate even if I asked. I decided not to push the matter. If it was important, he'd tell me. Right?

I couldn't help or ignore the way the hair on the

back of my neck rose, but I put it down to us being here, where maybe we shouldn't be. The last thing I wanted was for him to get a reprimand for bringing me here when he shouldn't. Would he get a slap on the wrist, or a fine? Maybe he'd get nothing more than a stern glance or a few words not to do it again.

"I'd be surprised if you were actually a hot mess," I said. "Hot, yes. Sometimes messy." I frowned again. I seemed to be digging myself into a hole here.

He grinned. "See? Hot mess. Just the way we both like it."

It wasn't more than half an hour since he fucked me up against the boards, but my clit still throbbed when he smiled. Especially when he looked at me the way he was right now.

"We should watch the movie." I reached for another slice of pizza. "This is nice."

"The pizza?" he asked.

"That too," I agreed. "And the wine. And the company. And this whole picnic. It's super sweet."

"I have a confession to make," he said. "Two of them in fact."

"Yes?" I asked tentatively.

Should I be worried about what he was about to say? In my experience, confessions usually didn't end well. I hoped to change that when Oliver and I confessed to Cat and Eden about what we were doing.

"Firstly, I am super sweet." He grinned and sipped

his wine. "Secondly, I really wanted to have a picnic under the stars, or take you to an outside concert. Maybe a drive-in movie, but there are none of those in Opal Springs. But then I realised, it's fucking cold outside. I figured this was a good compromise. I didn't want you to freeze your tits off."

"I don't want me to freeze my tits off either," I agreed. "Or your cock." I tilted my head and thought for a moment. "I wonder if cum can freeze. I mean, outside a specimen jar." Obviously frozen semen was nothing new.

"Excuse me if I don't try to find out," he said. "Ejaculating ice sounds painful as all hell." He grimaced.

I winced. "I'm not sure I want to know how it would feel if you came inside me like that." I won't say I wasn't curious, but that could go in my 'maybe' tray for another day.

"This is definitely a good compromise," I said finally. "It's like a private movie theatre. You really watch all the replays here?"

"Every one of them," he agreed. "I gotta admit, it took time for me to get used to watching and critiquing myself, but now I just do it." He shrugged one shoulder. "It helps me to visualise what I'm doing wrong and what I need to do right. In the heat of the moment, I sometimes don't know how the puck got past me. When I watch it back, it's obvious. I was too slow, or I didn't read their play correctly. It's always something.

I'll never stop working on it, not until I'm perfect. Since perfection is impossible, then I'll just keep doing what I'm doing."

"I've seen you on the ice," I said. "You're very impressive. One of the best goalies I've ever seen. Maybe even better than Phoenix DiMarco."

Toby's eyebrows twitched. "Maybe? Come on now, woman. I'm at least as good as he is."

I smiled teasingly. "The yardstick is pretty high. He is one of the top goalies in the country."

"He was until I landed here," Toby said with all his male, New York bravado. "Next time we play the Demons, I'm going to hand that motherfucker his ass."

I laughed. "I'm sure you will. I'll be right there cheering you on the whole time."

"You better be," he growled. "I want my woman there every time I play a home game."

A shiver went through me, sending a pulse straight to my core. "Your woman, hmmm?"

"Damn straight you are," he said firmly. "My woman. My girlfriend. *Mine*. I'm gonna keep on reminding you of that as long as it takes to sink into that pretty little head of yours." He placed his glass aside and leaned over to kiss my mouth.

"My boyfriend," I said against his lips.

"I like the sound of that." He deepened the kiss like he wanted to devour me from the outside in, piece by piece, until all that was left was a puddle on the blanket.

In the background, the movie played, while we explored each other's mouths, tasting and teasing, tongues dancing. Once I started kissing him, I didn't want to stop. I put my wine glass aside and wound my arms around him to pull him closer.

He lightly caressed my face, my cheek, my neck and throat. He moved his hand down slowly until it was resting on my hip. He made no move to remove my clothes or even get under them. For now, he just kissed me, his stubble rough against the smooth skin of my face.

I couldn't get enough of the way it felt, or the way he tasted. His plush lips were firm but gentle against mine, like he wanted to merge both of our bodies together, starting with our mouths. Like he wanted to kiss me until I was completely and utterly his. Claiming me.

I let him. I couldn't remember having ever just made out with a guy before. Tonight I did. Our bodies side-by-side, absorbing each other's warmth while we put everything into the kisses.

With every passing moment I felt more and more like this was exactly where I was meant to be. With him. With Oliver and Cole too, but right now this was about me and Toby. It felt like the universe put us right here, right now, together. He claimed me, but I claimed him as well. I could easily fall head over heels for him. With no regrets for doing it.

We finally broke off, both of us breathless, bodies

tangled around each other. My mouth must have been red from so much kissing.

I nestled into his arms and rested my ear against his chest. I closed my eyes and listened to the pounding of his heart. Rhythmic and soothing.

I sighed softly.

"What are you thinking?" He softly stroked my hair, his fingers tangling and untangling, over and over.

"I wasn't thinking anything," I confessed. "I was just enjoying the moment. You and me, being here right now. It feels right. But…"

His whole body stiffened. "Uh-oh, I don't like the sound of but," he said. "Am I that shitty a kisser?"

I tipped my face back to look at his, and smiled. "You're an amazing kisser. I was just going to say that if I'm not careful, I could fall for you."

"That's not a bad thing," he said. "I've already fallen for you."

"I'm scared," I confessed. "I'm scared of falling so hard and then having things go wrong."

"You're scared I'm going to break your heart?" he asked gently. "I can't promise I won't fuck up, but I can promise to try not to. I'd rather tear out my own heart than break yours. That's my promise to you. I'll do everything I can to keep your heart whole."

"I'll do the same," I said. "As long as we keep communicating, then maybe we all stand a chance of being together and being happy."

"I see no reason we can't be each other's forever," he said. He kissed the top of my head and squeezed me tighter.

"I'd like that," I said softly. Oliver, Toby and Cole. What more could one girl want?

CHAPTER 17

MARLEY

I glanced up from my computer screen as the surgery door opened.

Cole stepped inside, looking around tentatively. "Hey."

I shot to my feet. "Are you okay? The doctor is in with a patient at the moment but I can—"

"I'm fine," he said quickly. "I brought you something." He brought his hand out from behind his back and handed me a box of chocolates. "If they're not the kind you like, I can take them back and get something different."

I closed my hand over the box. "No, these are perfect. My favourites. Thank you."

To be honest if it started with 'choco' and ended with 'late,' it was my favourite. With the exception of chocolate covered ants. A girl has to draw the line somewhere.

He dropped his arm to his side. "That's great. I wasn't sure if you even ate chocolate. You could have been allergic for all I know." He looked adorably awkward.

I kissed his cheek and placed the box down on my desk. "Definitely not allergic, thank goodness. That might be worse than being allergic to alcohol." My curves were evidence of my enjoyment of both of those things.

He grimaced and leaned against the wall beside the desk, arms crossed over his burly chest. "That wouldn't be so bad in some ways."

My heart sank. "I'm so sorry. I didn't even think." Open mouth, insert foot right on in.

He responded with a minute shrug. "You couldn't have known. My father was worse when he was drunk."

"They often are," I said.

I'd seen it more times than I could count. Oliver donated as much time as he could, to the women's shelter in town, making sure victims got the support and medical care they needed. I spent a good deal of my time liaising between the shelter and the surgery, and being an ear for the women to talk to. The things they told me would give anyone nightmares.

Cole glanced down at the floor. "I suppose so. Losing inhibitions is a good way to bring out your inner asshole."

"Absolutely," I agreed. "Especially when your inner

asshole isn't buried all that deep." It sounded like Cole and Saxon's father wore his asshole right on the surface.

Cole looked back up. "Right. Anyway, I came to see if you're available for lunch? Today. Now. Or soon, or… Unless you've already eaten."

"No," I replied. "I mean, I haven't already eaten. As a matter of fact, I was just about to take a lunch break, so your timing is perfect."

"Good." He nodded. "Do you need to—" He nodded in the direction of the treatment room.

"Ask permission to go to lunch with you?" I asked, only half-joking.

Cole's face turned slightly pink and a hint of anger flashed in his eyes. "If he's that possessive that you can't even go to lunch with someone else…"

"He's not," I said quickly. "I mean, not entirely. But he knows about you and he's okay with it. As my boss, I should let him know if I'm stepping out of the office, that's all."

Something crossed Cole's face, but I couldn't put a finger on what it was before it was gone.

"Yeah, okay, I get that," he said. "I forgot you worked for him for a minute. Do you need to wait and take money from the patient?"

"No." I picked up my phone and bag. "The person he's seeing is someone who doesn't have to pay. Some-times he takes on people who can't afford to see a doctor. It's something he likes to do for Opal Springs. He's always trying to take care of the whole town."

"That's commendable," Cole said. "It seems like he wants what's best for everyone."

"He does." I tapped on the treatment room door and called out that I was going to lunch. In reply I got a muffled, "Okay."

I turned back around to see Cole's eyes dipped, midway down my body. He must have been checking out my ass. Next time, I'd be sure to give it a wiggle.

"Where do you want to go?" I asked. "There's a nice little coffee shop three doors down."

"If that's where you want to go, let's go there." He slipped his hand into mine and pushed out the door and onto the street. "I didn't have any particular plans beyond asking you out. I tend not to plan too far ahead."

"Me either," I said. His hand felt warm and firm in mine, like we fit together perfectly. "You never know what the day will bring, much less weeks and months from now. I prefer to live in the moment."

In that way, I was very different from Cat. She had her life planned out since we were in school. Of course, she hadn't planned to have three boyfriends, but she'd decided in year two to become a vet. She was going to fit that in between speed skating, and that was exactly what she did for a long time.

Me? I had a hard enough time trying to decide what outfit to wear from one day to the next.

"Me too," Cole said. He gestured for me to step through the open doorway into the coffee shop ahead of him. "Especially before the Ghouls joined the AIHL. That was like being in limbo for a couple of years."

"That sounds painful," I remarked.

He flashed me a smile, showing dimples in both cheeks. "Both literal and figurative limbo for would be. I've only done the figurative kind. That was bad enough."

"You've never done the limbo?" I glanced over my shoulder at him while I picked up two menus and handed one to him. "You don't know what you're missing."

He leaned in to whisper in my ear. "I prefer to bend than to be bent."

My mouth formed an O and heat rushed to my face. "I kinda like bending."

"I know." His breath was warm against my cheek. He took the menu and started to look it over.

I swallowed hard. "I think I'll have a grilled cheese and tomato sandwich and a cup of coffee."

"Me too." He took back my menu, handed it to the server and ordered for us both. The server handed him a table number and some napkins.

"I could have paid for my own," I said.

He led me over to a table in the corner and pulled out the chair for me. "I like to be a gentleman sometimes."

I sat down and placed my bag at my feet. "Gentleman in the street, ghoul in the sheets?"

He sat beside me and snorted a soft laugh. "Something like that." He hesitated for a moment before saying, "About the other day."

"I meant what I said when I told you I enjoyed it," I said. "I haven't changed my mind. I don't plan on changing it anytime soon."

His shoulders dropped in relief. "I was thinking we could go out tomorrow night."

"Why do I think there's more to that than just a nice dinner and a movie?" I asked.

His tongue slid through the gap between his slightly parted lips. He pressed them together and swallowed.

"I was thinking we could…take it a step further. If there's something you've ever fantasised about, maybe we could…act it out." He sat back to let the server place our coffees in front of us.

"As in, you doing whatever you want with me, and me letting you?" A surge of excitement passed through me. "I'd like that. It happens I've always had this one recurring fantasy."

I was awoken by the sound of the window sliding open. I'd left it unlocked, but it still startled me. I sat up in bed and looked around, reorienting myself.

"Hello?" I called out softly.

The only response was the window being pushed open further and a dark figure climbing inside.

A shiver of excitement passed through me.

He moved towards the bed and grabbed me, a hand going over my mouth. Strong arms pulled me up to my feet and over to the door.

He smelled like spices and arousal. He was already getting off on this.

Good, because so was I.

I caught sight of the outline of his face in the street-light that came through the open window.

"Open the door," he growled softly. He pushed me towards it.

I pushed back against him, but he held me hard, shoving me forward again. I grabbed the handle and pushed it down before pulling the door open.

He dragged me over to the front of the house and over to the front door. This one, he opened himself before pulling me out into the night and over to his car.

As we'd figured out in advance, he pulled open the back door and shoved me inside onto the seat. I'd insisted he not put me in the boot of the car. For some reason, that made me uncomfortable.

I flopped down face first on the back seat. My hands under me, I started to push myself up.

He placed a hand on my back and pressed me back down. He grabbed the waistband of my pyjama pants and yanked them down and off. He tossed them onto the base of the seat, right beside me and slapped his hand down hard on my ass.

I jumped slightly and squealed. Fuck, that felt so good.

Again, I tried to push myself up, but he held me down and slapped my ass several more times, until my cheeks must have been pink.

Panting, I flopped forward. He grabbed my ankles and shoved my feet into the car before closing the door behind me.

I lay there half-naked while he slid into the driver's seat and pulled the car away from my house.

I had no idea where he was taking me, he just said he knew a place. I lay still and tried to relax while he drove for several minutes.

When the car stopped again, he climbed out and wrenched open the back door. He leaned in and grabbed my hand, pulling me out far enough to be able to throw me over his shoulder.

I wriggled and writhed as though trying to get away.

He brought another stinging slap down on my ass and carried me through a stand of trees to a small, rundown house. He opened the door without a key and lowered me onto the old, scratched hardwood floor.

Immediately, I got onto all fours and started to crawl away.

He grabbed my ankle and dragged me back to him. My pyjama top rose up as he pulled, sliding over my breasts, to my armpits. He gripped the hem and yanked it up over my head, using my shirt to pin my arms while his other hand forced my legs open and rammed his fingers into my soaking pussy.

I moaned. I couldn't pretend I wasn't enjoying everything he was doing to me. He was driving me absolutely wild. Wilder still, when without warning he pulled his fingers out of me and rammed his cock all the way inside. I hadn't even known he'd undone his pants.

I cried out in pain, pleasure and surprise. Cried out again when he pounded harder into me than any man had ever done before. He held absolutely nothing back.

This was the real Cole. The animal under the shy, civilised exterior. The creature he made no effort to contain, because I gave him permission to let himself loose. To use every centimetre of my body the way he wanted to.

He pulled out of me, rolled me over and scooted up just far enough to shove his cock between my lips. He tasted of his own arousal and mine, a heady combination.

"Take every bit of me," he growled. "Choke on my cock." He wrapped a hand around my throat, holding me while he relentlessly fucked my mouth.

I took him in as deep as I could, gagging with each of his furious thrusts.

He squeezed my throat a little tighter, until my vision started to blur. His other hand, he tangled in my hair, tugging until it hurt.

As quickly as he had with my pussy, he pulled himself out of my mouth, straddled my body and rammed back into me.

"Fucking hell," he grinned. "I'm going to cum inside you and you're going to take all of it. Understood?"

I whimpered as though I wasn't completely into every moment of this.

He groaned again. "Holy shit. Do that again."

I whimpered a couple more times and struggled against him while he held me in place and fucked me hard. The last whimper turned into a shout as I came violently. I felt as though my body wasn't mine, like I'd entered some universe where nothing existed but pleasure and pain. The perfect partnership of bliss.

Cole came while I was still mid-orgasm, shouting his own release and pounding harder before he went still, giving me every drop of his release.

He finally sagged over me, loosening his grip on my throat and hair.

"Marley," he whispered.

"Cole," I whispered back. "That was amazing."

"You don't hate me?" Even now, he was uncertain. Even after everything we'd discussed. We'd planned almost every moment of this and he'd followed it to the letter. How could I hate him?

"I don't hate you at all," I said. "This was a fantasy come true. Everything was perfect."

"Thank fuck." He exhaled softly. "For me too." He rolled over until we lay side-by-side, his cock still embedded inside me. "Thank you. Thank you for not judging me on this. For letting me be me."

"Thank you for the exact same things," I whispered.

"Another guy might think I'm crazy for wanting to do this. Not you."

"Did I hurt you?" he asked.

"A little bit," I said. "I'm going to wear every bruise with pride."

"Shit," he said softly. "I shouldn't think it's hot that I'm going to see bruises I left on you."

"Yes, you should," I said. "It is hot." I meant that. Every one would be a sign that we could be ourselves and act out our fantasies because we were comfortable enough with each other to do it. That was everything.

"Then…I should leave some more."

CHAPTER 18

OLIVER

"You look tired, are you getting enough sleep?" I peered over Marley's desk at her.

"Probably not." She cracked the seal on a bottle of water and took a sip. "Between going to games, the pub, dates and everything in between, I haven't had time to breathe for the last month."

I pulled over another chair and sat down near her. Close enough that I could almost touch her, but not so close that if anyone walked through the door they'd ask questions.

Sneaking around was beyond frustrating at this point. Cat was due to have her baby in another month. Then all of this could end, once and for all. I could start a life with the woman I loved, and her other boyfriends.

"I feel as though I should give you more time off," I said. "I could get someone in if you need a break." I watched her carefully. I was almost certain she wasn't just busy or overworked. I pushed down the small bubble of hope, for now. The time to think about that would come.

She screwed the lid back onto the bottle and set it aside beside her computer.

"I'm okay, really. Just a bit tired today. Maybe I'll have an early night tonight." She glanced over at me and sighed.

"I know." I placed a hand over one of hers. "We shouldn't still be dancing this dance. It's only for a little while longer."

"Is it?" She cocked her head at me. "Sometimes I worry you'll find another excuse not to tell everyone we're together."

"Marley—" I started.

She shook her head. "I'm sorry, I shouldn't snap at you." She massaged her temples with her thumb and middle finger. "I just feel like it's never going to happen."

"It will." I squeezed her hand. "I promise I am not, in any way, looking for any further reasons to keep our relationship a secret. Quite the opposite. If I had one of those devices to make time go faster, I'd use it. Short of inducing Cat against her will, there's nothing I can do."

I won't lie, I'd considered doing that, but there was no way I could do it without potentially endangering her, her baby and our relationship. Some things were better left alone. I knew plenty of other doctors who would have played God, but I wasn't doing that, not with my daughter. Not even if it meant being with Marley sooner. The wait was almost killing me. Especially now, when I suspected Toby, Cole and I had done what I hoped for.

"Please don't do anything like that," Marley said. She turned her hand around under mine and laced our fingers together. "I know you wouldn't. You adore her." She looked like she was going to add something, but glanced down at our entwined fingers instead.

"What is it?" I pressed gently.

She shook her head slightly. "It's silly."

"Marley-Jane, there's nothing you could say that I wouldn't take seriously," I said. "I love you. You're the woman I want to spend the rest of my life with. Whatever you're thinking, it's important to me. Even if you're only deciding between vanilla latte and caramel latte." Of which, she probably shouldn't be drinking either, but I couldn't mention that right now.

She blinked a couple of times, eyes glazed. "You love me?"

I smiled softly. "Of course I love you. I've loved you for a long time. Now, tell me, what's on your mind?"

"I love you too," she said. She swallowed visibly. "I was thinking about what happens after. When we can finally be together in public."

"We live happily ever after," I said. "You and me, Toby, Cole, Lucifer the cat and Stanley the goldfish. And whatever other pets you want."

"What if I don't want any more pets?" she asked.

"You don't have to have pets," I said. "Pets are definitely optional."

"What about children?" she blurted. "Would you ever want more of those, or is it enough to have the two you already have?"

I contained a smile and looked at her through my lowered brows. "Do you want children?"

Her tongue darted tantalisingly over her full lower lip. I'd like her to do that to my cock, but this conversation was more important right now.

"I want children someday," she said finally. "When everything has settled down. I was just worried you might not. You still haven't answered."

"I haven't, have I?" I rubbed my chin. "Nothing would make me happier than to give you everything you want, including kids. You'd look absolutely beautiful with a big baby bump." Preferably sooner than 'someday.'

"You wouldn't mind being a father again?" she asked tentatively.

I'd love nothing more than to be a father to her children, but I'd settle for her being pregnant, regardless of the paternity.

"I wouldn't mind if you had Toby's or Cole's baby, or mine," I said. "Whoever the father was, I'd love any baby of yours as much as I love you. I'd think of them as mine, no matter what."

I was, after all, the one engineering all of this. If I hadn't changed her birth control pills for sugar tablets, making her pregnant would be much more difficult, if not impossible. My tampering made way for us to put a baby in her belly. I was as much a part of this as they were. Maybe more so, because I allowed them to be with her and fuck her. To fill her beautiful pussy with their cum.

"How did I get so lucky?" Marley asked. "You've always been so sweet and supportive. You'll make an incredible father again, when the time comes."

She sighed out her nose. "Cat is going to lose her mind, isn't she? Us getting together is going to be diffi-cult enough for her to accept without the thought of me giving birth to her sibling. And being grandmother to her baby."

"Cat will deal with it," I said. She'd have no choice. This was about Marley, me, Toby and Cole.

"What if she can't?" Marley asked. "What if she insists you choose between me and her?" She looked genuinely scared.

"Then I'll have to work harder to convince her," I said easily. "I'm not giving you up, Marley-Jane. Not now. Not ever. You belong to me. We have a future to live together."

I scooted the chair over closer. I looked her in the eye, then placed a hand on her still flat belly.

"One day, this will swell with our baby. I intend to be there for every moment of that, regardless of what Cat thinks or believes. Her baby and any baby of ours will grow up together. They won't care if they're aunts or uncles or whatever the hell. All they'll know is they'll have a friend who is also family."

She glanced down at my hand. "They'll probably be too far apart in age to want to play together, but I hope they get along. Honestly, I'm not sure I'll be ready for at least a couple more years. Everything is still so new and fragile. I want to make sure I have even, solid ground under my feet before a baby comes along."

"If you wait until the right moment, it will never come," I said. "Babies come along when they want to."

Especially when their mother is no longer on birth control. It was fortunate she never would have thought to question me when I gave her the box of sugar pills. She would have just taken them like the sweet, trusting woman she was. Her innocence was one of the things that endeared her to me the most. She wasn't jaded like me and most people my age. If I had my way, she never would be. I'd love to put her in a box and keep her safe and sound from the world.

There was no way she'd let me, she was too independent for that, but I'd still do my best to protect her as much as I could.

"Any baby can wait a little bit longer," she said. "Don't worry, I'm careful with my birth control. You know me, I've never been a big fan of surprises."

"I love surprises," I said. "I don't know what I love more, being on the receiving end or the giving one." I rubbed my chin again. "I think I love giving them the most. I've always preferred to give presents than receive them. Especially orgasms."

She smiled. "You don't seem to mind when I give those to you."

"I don't mind at all," I said. "But I love to see you writhe and moan when I fuck you with my hand, mouth, or my cock. Watching you come is one of my favourite things in the world."

Her little breathy groans were the most beautiful music I ever heard. If I had my way, I'd give her a hundred orgasms a day, just to hear that sound.

"You're going to make me ruin my panties." She glanced towards the door.

I smiled. "Good. They should be permanently ruined. Although, it would be better if you wore none at all."

She arched an eyebrow at me. "Oh, really?"

I leaned in closer. "Really."

No longer caring who might walk through the door, I placed my hands on her knees and turned her to face me. Eyes on hers, I slid the tips of my fingers under the hem of her skirt. Moving with torturous slowness, I slipped my hands up further until I could hook my fingers around the waistband of her panties. I gripped them tight and pulled them down.

She lifted her ass off the chair, high enough for me to pull her panties off and down her thighs.

I pulled them past her knees and over her calves to

drop to the floor. I raised one foot, then the other and pulled the scrap of black lace free.

Triumphantly, I pushed her panties into my pocket.

"We should have more patients coming soon. While I'm seeing them, I'll be thinking of you spending the rest of your day sitting out here with a bare pussy." My cock was going to throb like a bitch before the day was over.

"Yes, Doctor," she said sweetly. "I'm going to be as wet as hell by the time the last patient leaves."

I bit back a groan. This woman was going to be the end of me in the best possible way.

"Good," I said. "Because I'm going to fill that pretty little pussy with my cock and fuck you hard right there on your desk after that door is locked behind them."

"Yes please," she whispered. "I'll be looking forward to it."

I sat back just as the door opened and the first of the afternoon patients stepped inside.

It was going to be a long, hard afternoon.

CHAPTER 19
MARLEY

Tap. Tap. Tap.

"MJ! Are you nearly finished in there?"

Tap. Tap. Tap.

"Almost, Mum," I called back over my shoulder.

I pushed myself up to my feet and flushed the toilet. My stomach turned again, but I took the couple of steps to the sink and rinsed my mouth with toothpaste and water from the tap. I wiped a towel over my mouth and unlocked the bathroom door.

"You look like crap," she said. She cocked her head at me in concern.

"Thanks," I said sarcastically. "I feel like crap." I hadn't been able to keep anything down all morning. Not even a piece of dry toast.

"You're calling in sick from work, aren't you?" she asked. "No point taking whatever you've got to work and spreading it around." She kept a safe distance. As if gastrointestinal viruses were airborne.

"I'll give it a few more minutes," I said. "It was probably something I ate. No big deal. I'll be fine."

She looked sceptical, but didn't argue.

"You're not pregnant are you?" she asked. "I've seen those boys of yours. They seem like…red-blooded men to me."

That was a roundabout way of saying she knew I was fucking them. She was another person Oliver and I were keeping the truth about our relationship from. Unlike just about everyone else, she wouldn't be angry at me for keeping it a secret. She'd probably say she knew it all along. Maybe she did.

"Of course not," I said. "Do you need to use the bathroom?"

"Yes I do." She hurried inside and closed the door behind her. Sharing one bathroom with a house full of other adults got old a long time ago, but it was what it was. Someday soon, I'd move out, and Mum and Dad would have the bathroom to themselves.

I slipped into my bedroom and considered what she asked me. I was quick to dismiss it, but now I gave it more thought, I wasn't so sure. Birth control wasn't one hundred percent effective, even if you're as careful with it as I was.

My head spun with the implications. What would any of my boyfriends think if I was pregnant? Oliver would be all right with it, but the timing wasn't the best. As for Toby and Cole, I could only guess how they might respond.

How did I even feel about the possibility? I wasn't ready to try to get my head around it. I needed to know for sure.

I should ask Oliver to take blood for a proper confirmation, but I wasn't ready to go to him with this yet. Part of me was worried how he'd react, given we couldn't even tell Cat about us yet, much less a baby.

"What a fucking mess," I said under my breath. And in the next one, "Calm down, Marley. It was probably just the chicken you ate yesterday."

In case it wasn't, I grabbed up my bag and slipped out the door like I was doing something wrong. Like somehow my mother might follow me out, shaking her finger at me.

It was only a five minute walk to the shops to buy a pregnancy test before returning home. By the time I got back, my stomach had settled somewhat.

"Probably a false alarm," I muttered as I let myself back into the house. I'd worked for Oliver long enough to know sometimes people had symptoms for no obvious reason.

Still, I slipped into the now empty bathroom and quickly took the test. I lowered the toilet seat and sat down to watch the window on the plastic stick.

One pink line to confirm the test was working properly.

Two pink lines to confirm…

"Fuck."

"You look like crap." Eden slid into the seat opposite me.

"That seems to be the consensus today, yes," I said. "I'll do my best to look less shitty from now on."

She dipped her head. "I'm sorry. I meant you look tired and you obviously need to talk about something. You sounded upset on the phone. Is everything okay?"

I exhaled slowly and ignored my twisting stomach. It wasn't as bad now as it was this morning, but my anxiety was a lot higher. I'd ended up going to work, but Oliver was at the hospital, leaving the other GPs to work in the surgery. For once, that was a blessing. I didn't think I could keep myself from blurting it out to him, and I needed to get my head around it first.

"I don't know," I said slowly. "I mean, no, but I didn't know who else to turn to."

She put a hand on my wrist and squeezed gently. "You know you can tell me anything, right? What are friends for? Whatever's going on, I won't judge you. Promise."

She might not make that promise if she knew the full extent of what was happening in my life. She might hate me instead, but I needed to get this off my chest.

"I'm pregnant," I whispered. Saying it out loud like

that made it seem all the more real. Way too fucking real.

Her eyes widened and she started to smile. "That's fantastic. Isn't it?" Her smile faded to a concerned frown.

"I'm not sure," I admitted. "I haven't told anyone else yet. I don't know how they're going to respond."

"Do you know..." She looked like she was trying to think how to finish that question.

"Exactly who the father is?" I asked. "No, I don't. I don't know how any... Either of them will take it." For now, I had to let her believe I could only have Toby or Cole's baby growing inside me. That situation was complicated enough as it was.

"How do you want them to take it?" she asked.

"I—" I hadn't thought about that. How *did* I want them to respond? Obviously, I didn't want them to freak out and run away. That would be the worst thing they could do. They'd made it clear they wanted to be with me, but this might change everything.

"I want them to be happy about it," I said finally. "I want them to want to be with me the way Cat's boyfriends are. I want them to accept this baby as their own, no matter what. But if they can't do that, I'll have no choice but to understand and let them go."

My heart ached at the possibility.

"Then you need to tell them," she said. "Give them the chance to figure out how they feel and what they want to do going forward. They have a while to figure it out, right?"

"I guess so. I can't be that far along." If I was, there'd be no doubt over who the father of my baby was. Before Toby and Cole, there was only Oliver. That would certainly have simplified the matter, but I was almost certain that wasn't the case.

"So sit them down, and tell them," Eden said, like it was the easiest thing in the world. "They both care about you. They'll probably be ecstatic. Why wouldn't they be? This is exciting. I'm so happy for you. Just think, your baby and Cat's can grow up together. I bet they'll be as thick as thieves."

"Yeah, I'm sure they will be," I said. Ironic that Oliver and I were talking about that just a couple of days ago. I could be carrying her sibling as we spoke.

"Of course they will," Eden said. "I think we need to celebrate over a cup of coffee. Can I get you one?"

"Maybe just juice," I said. I'd have to cut down on coffee for the next few months. That was going to suck. Although, right now, that was the least of my worries. "Thank you." I managed a watery smile.

"Of course." She pushed her seat back and stood. "Anything for our newest mummy." She grinned before slipping away through the tables towards the coffee shop counter.

"Mummy," I mouthed to myself. I kept my hands on the table to keep them from straying to my belly. Nothing would give me away faster if someone I knew walked through the door. That didn't stop my mind from straying. Growing inside me was a tiny life that would someday call me Mummy. I'd have to get all of the baby things at some point. A stroller, baby clothes, everything.

No part of this felt real

I dropped my face to my hands and shook my head. This could all very easily become overwhelming. I was starting to understand what Oliver meant when he said that no one was ever ready to have babies. I certainly wasn't.

"You okay?" Eden set a glass of juice down in front of me and slipped back into her chair to sip her coffee. The smell made my stomach turn.

I lifted my face. "I don't know how to answer that question. I'm mostly okay but partly completely terrified." I thought about that for a moment. "Actually, I think that's the other way around. I'm partly okay but mostly terrified."

"You wouldn't be human if you weren't feeling a lot of conflicting emotions," Eden said. "This is a lot to process, but you will. It seems like a lot now, but when the guys know and you've gotten used to the idea, you'll start to get excited."

"Are you sure you're not a therapist?" I teased. "You're very good at knowing the right things to say."

She smiled. "I watch a lot of those talk shows. Sometimes they make sense."

"You mean the ones where people argue over who

might be the father of someone's baby. Then they do a DNA test. Then people start throwing chairs." I grimaced.

She laughed. "Something like that, but your life will *not* turn out that way. Besides, I can't imagine Toby and Cole throwing chairs at each other. They seem to get along pretty well."

"They do," I agreed. "At the moment they do. What if I tell them and everything changes between them? They could end up hating each other because of me."

If that happened, it would break my heart. I cared about them and I knew they cared about each other. To see that end would be devastating. To know I was the cause of it, I wasn't sure if I'd be able to forgive myself. Would they forgive me?

"Do you really think that's likely?" she asked.

I picked up my juice and took a sip. "I suppose not, but that's another thing to worry about until I can talk to them. They may decide they don't want to share."

Oliver in particular might decide that. Sharing me was one thing. Sharing a baby was another. It was almost funny how I thought the situation was complicated before.

My whole life felt like a ticking time bomb, ready to explode. I wasn't sure what would happen when the dust started to settle. Would it settle? I hope it would, otherwise I'd be raising this baby by myself.

CHAPTER 20
MARLEY

Knock. Knock. Knock.

I almost jumped out of my skin when someone tapped on the car window beside me. Heart in my throat, I twisted around to see Toby standing on the other side of the glass.

He grinned and opened the door. "Didn't mean to scare the shit out of you. You looked like you were lost in thought."

"I was." I snatched my bag and phone from the seat beside me and climbed out of the car. How long I'd been sitting there, I didn't know. Long enough. I considered driving away several times, but hadn't been able to bring myself to do it. I couldn't, this was too important.

I went to give Toby a quick kiss, but he gripped my shoulder and deepened it. Our lips and tongues slid together like they were made for each other. I could easily have dragged him back into the car and fucked him here in broad daylight. On another day, maybe I would. But not today.

"Save some of that for me," Cole said from behind Toby.

Laughing, Toby broke off and turned to kiss Cole as deeply as he'd kissed me.

Fuck that was hot.

Cole pressed the heel of his hand to the back of Toby's neck and kissed him back like he wanted to eat the other player alive.

Eventually, Cole broke off the kiss and grabbed me to devour my lips.

"Are you coming in, or are you going to make out all day instead?" Oliver called from where he stood on the front steps of his house.

"Make out," Toby called back, laughing. "You jealous, old man?"

"Absolutely I am," Oliver said. "All of you get your asses in here." He stepped back and gestured us inside.

With Cole holding one of my hands and Toby the other, we stepped up the driveway and into the house.

The moment the door closed behind us, Oliver's mouth was on mine, his hands on my hips.

If I wasn't careful, I'd forget why I asked them to meet me here. Instead we could strip each other naked and fuck all over the house. That sounded like much more fun than having a serious, adult conversation.

I placed my hands on Oliver's chest and pushed him back gently.

"That wasn't what I came here for," I said regretfully.

"You look very serious, Marley-Jane," he said.

I sighed softly. "I am. Let's go in and sit down."

With them looking at me in concern, we moved into the living room. I sat down on the couch, my three men arrayed around me. Each one looked good enough to eat. Either I was the luckiest girl on earth, or I was about to be the most heartbroken.

Oliver sat on my left side. He took my hand and looked me in the eyes. "You know there's nothing you can say to us that we can't deal with."

"Unless she wants to end it," Cole said softly.

"That's not going to happen," Toby said. He seemed sure of that.

"When you hear what I have to say, you might want to end it," I said.

"Still not going to happen," Toby said.

"Absolutely not," Oliver said.

"What they said," Cole agreed. "I'm invested in this. In us." He gestured at himself, then at me and Toby. To Oliver, he gave a short nod.

"Me too," Toby said. He placed his hands to either side of him on the chair and leaned towards me. "What is it, sweetheart?"

Over and over, I'd thought about how to tell them this. A thousand scenarios had run through my head from beginning to end. Some ending well, others ending badly. I'd told them quickly and I'd told them slowly. None of it helped decide how to actually say the words. I'd even considered telling them by text, but dismissed that quickly enough.

I exhaled out my nose.

"I just want to start by saying I'm sorry and I don't know how it happened. I mean, I do, but..." I shook my head.

"Did you sleep with someone else?" Oliver was frowning at me.

"No," I said quickly. "The three of you give me everything I need. I can't even imagine being interested in anyone else." Things were tangled enough as they were without adding anyone else into the equation.

"So, what is it?" Cole pressed gently. "Like Oliver said, there's nothing you can say that would drive us away."

"I'm pregnant," I blurted out.

Heavy silence hung in the air for a dozen lifetimes. My words sank in one by one, but the response wasn't what I was expecting. All three of them grinned. Not just grinned, but looked smugly pleased with themselves.

"That's awesome," Oliver said finally. "You're going to be an absolutely incredible mother."

"Absolutely are," Toby agreed. "The best ever."

"The very best," Cole said softly. His response was the hardest to gauge. He seemed uneasy, but happy. Conflicted, definitely.

I looked around at each of their faces. "You don't seem surprised."

Of course, Oliver saw how tired I was. Maybe he suspected something like this was up. I was surprised he hadn't asked anything. Maybe he was giving me time to figure things out for myself.

"What we are, is happy and excited," Oliver said. "We knew you wanted to have a baby. We wanted to have one with you. I didn't think it would happen so quickly, but we'll be ready."

I looked around at them again. Something was going on here, but I couldn't quite figure out what.

"I don't understand," I said slowly. "What do you mean? You knew I wanted to have a baby? You didn't think it would happen quickly? I don't—" I shook my head.

Oliver squeezed my hand. "We saw what you wanted and made sure you got it." Like it was nothing more than that.

I stared at him. "You made sure... How?" I felt the blood drain from my face. "What did you do?"

Without any hint of apology, he said, "I changed your birth control pills. The packet I gave you was just made of sugar. Toby and Cole agreed—"

My face whipped around to stare at both of them. "They agreed to what?"

Cole was looking down at his feet, but Toby met my gaze.

"To help get you pregnant," he said. "To fuck you and put a baby inside you."

I must be hearing things. I sat completely still for at

least a minute or two, trying to wrap my head around what they were saying.

"You tampered with my birth control so you could get me pregnant without my knowledge or consent?" I asked slowly. That couldn't be what he was saying, could it? Was I asleep and having a nightmare? If I was, I'd like to wake up right now.

I didn't wake up.

Cole looked back up. At least he had the grace to look uncomfortable. Not ashamed, but awkward, like he wanted to step back when tensions got too high.

"We did it because we knew you wanted a baby," Oliver said. "I've seen the way you look at Cat and her belly. I love you, I wanted to make that dream come true for you. For all of us." He waved a hand over toward Toby and Cole.

What the absolute, ever loving fuck? I'd heard some twisted shit in my life, but nothing like this. Nothing even close.

I buried my face in my hands. I couldn't even begin to imagine what Cat was going to say when she found out about all of this. I didn't even know what to say about it myself.

I looked back up. "You love me enough to do something like this? To go behind my back and make decisions about my body without my knowledge? Do you have any idea how violated I feel right now?"

I shoved my glasses back up my nose. It didn't help to clear the haze of tears. "I feel as though you've all raped me. You might as well have. You've violated my body and my trust. Worse, you've done that to an innocent child, who deserves better than to come into this world this way."

Tears were sliding down my cheeks and dripping onto my blouse. I felt sicker than I had when I was throwing up into the toilet. I wanted to vomit every meal I'd ever had.

I looked around at these three men and all I saw were three strangers. Three guys I thought I knew, but clearly I didn't know them at all. They obviously didn't know me. If they did, they would have known not to take a choice like this out of my hands.

"I understand this is overwhelming," Oliver said. "Give it some time. When it fully sinks in, you'll realise what we did, we did because we love you. We love the child growing inside you. You will too. Knowing you, you already do."

He actually had the nerve to smile softly, like he completely believed what he was saying and he'd done something beautiful. He was out of his fucking mind, or I was.

I barely recognised him. He looked like Oliver, but clearly there was a monster lurking just under the surface. How deep did that really go? I'd completely misjudged him. Toby and Cole as well.

They must have had a good laugh at my expense. Did they rub their hands together when they hatched this plan to get me pregnant? Did they talk about it over a few beers? Did they plan how they'd come inside me until one of their sperm slid inside my fertile egg? How long had all of this been going on anyway? Was getting together with Toby and Cole coincidence or had Oliver engineered all of this from the beginning?

Everything I thought I knew was a lie. They'd all grabbed hold of the rug and pulled it straight out from under my feet. And they'd enjoyed every moment of it.

"You don't know me at all." I pulled my hand away from him and got to my feet. "I'm starting to think you don't know anything about me. If you did, you wouldn't do something like this to me. This is not something someone does when they love someone else. This is… I don't even know what this is. It's wrong. It's horrible. I can't believe you'd do this to me and not care how I feel about it."

"Of course we care." Cole got to his feet and took half a step towards me. "We did it because we care." His voice was soft and low, almost soothing.

Any other time, I might have fallen for it, but right now it sounded like so many poisonous words. This whole situation was beyond fucked up and toxic. I was living in a nightmare.

"You did it because you wanted me pregnant," I snarled. "You wanted to be the ones to decide that for me. To have control over me. That ends right now. None of you will have control over me or my baby. You have no say over anything I do. I don't want to see you or have anything to do with any of you ever again."

"You don't mean that," Oliver said. "You need to calm down, Marley-Jane." He put a hand out towards me.

I jerked away.

"Don't call me that," I snapped. "You don't get to call me that ever again. I quit. I quit my job and I quit us. We are *done*."

I ran over to the door, wrenched it open and hurried through before slamming it shut behind me. I pulled open the door to my car and all but threw myself inside before starting the engine.

Blinking away a haze of tears, I peeled the car away from the curb and drove, not caring where I was going or where I'd end up.

CHAPTER 21
TOBY

"That went well," I said sarcastically. I crossed my arms over my chest and lifted my chin in Oliver's direction. "I've seen clusterfucks in my day, but that takes the cake."

Oliver rolled his eyes. "She'll be fine. Once she calms down, she'll realise we were right. She'll be excited for that baby."

"Are you sure about that?" Cole asked. "She seemed pretty upset. I can't blame her. What we did was—" He shook his head slowly.

"The right thing to do," Oliver said. "Like I told her, we did nothing more than give her what she wanted. Now she has that, she just needs to realise it. Give her a day or two, she'll be fine."

Cole didn't look reassured. If anything, he looked more unsettled. He massaged his temples with the tips of his fingers, a deep frown etched on his forehead.

"What if she isn't?" I had to voice what Cole and I were both thinking. "She seemed pretty certain when she said she didn't want to see any of us ever again. What happens then? She's going to disappear forever and we won't get to see our baby?"

As far as I was concerned, the baby was mine. Biologically or otherwise. I was going to be a part of their life. Whatever it took for that to happen, I'd do it. Marley and I would raise this baby together. There was no question of me taking them from her. Unless Marley wanted nothing to do with the kid, then they'd have at least two parents.

For the first time, a flicker of uncertainty crossed Oliver's face. "That won't happen."

The set of his jaw suggested he wouldn't allow it to happen. Would he try to take the baby away from her? He'd have one hell of a fight on his hands if he did. From Marley and from me. He clearly liked to be in control, but he didn't get whatever he wanted just because he said so. Fuck that.

"You don't know that." I shook my head. "You have no real way of telling whether that was the last time any of us will see her. We should go after her."

I should have done that immediately. Oliver told us to let her go and I shouldn't have listened. Shouldn't have let her get in her car and drive away. Even if I had to hold her down, I should have found a way to keep her here. In the mood she was in right now, she could do herself some real and permanent damage. Hopefully she was in her right mind enough to drive carefully.

"Where would she go?" Cole asked. He seemed to have come to the same conclusion. She shouldn't be there on her own.

"Under other circumstances, she would have come to me," Oliver said. "Now, I wouldn't hazard a guess." He squeezed his eyes shut for a few moments before opening them again. From the expression on his face, he was considering a bunch of alternatives and concluding that he had no clear answers. Apparently he didn't know her as well as he thought he did.

"Then we call her." Without waiting for them to respond, I pulled out my phone and pressed on her number. To the surprise of absolutely no one, she didn't answer. I left a message, but all I could think to say was, "Hey, call me back. Please."

I shoved my phone back into the pocket of my jeans, knowing it was unlikely she'd call me back anytime soon. That didn't mean I wouldn't keep trying. I'd call her back again in half an hour or so. And I would keep calling until I spoke to her. I didn't like to be ignored and I wasn't going to start now. No matter how hurt she was.

"What do we do now?" Cole looked like a lost boy.

I draped an arm over his shoulders and gave him a squeeze. I was tempted to say we kick Oliver's ass, and then do just that, but it was unlikely to help rectify the situation. It would, however, make me feel a fuck ton better.

"This was a stupid idea," I said. "We never should have agreed to go behind her back. Even if everything ends well, she's never gonna forget today. She doesn't deserve to feel the way she's feeling right now. She should be happy and excited, and here with us so we can spoil her rotten. She shouldn't be out there by herself dealing with all those big feelings."

I was struggling hard enough with those emotions. I wanted to be excited about the baby, but instead I was worried I'd ruined the best thing that ever happened to me.

"You're right, it was a bad idea," Cole said. "It was all kinds of fucked up."

"What does it say about you that you agreed to it?" Oliver asked us both. "Don't deny that you wanted this as much as I did. It wasn't just about giving her what she wanted, it was about being in control. Showing her we own her. Both of you wanted to be the one to get her pregnant. I'm willing to bet almost anything both of you wanted to beat out the other. To be the one to knock her up." He raised an eyebrow in challenge.

I glanced at Cole, then back to Oliver.

"Fine," I said. "You're right. I did want to be the one to put a baby in her belly. That doesn't make any of this right. Doesn't make it any less fucked up. We should have waited until she was good and fucking ready."

"Who knows how long that would have taken?"

Oliver said. "Not to mention the fact birth control fails all the time. She could have become pregnant anyway. We have no way of predicting any of that."

"If it was a genuine accident, we wouldn't have lied to her and gone behind her back," Cole said softly. He glanced down at the floor. "Maybe we should have told her that was what this was. Just an accident." His sigh was heavy and laced with regret and anger at himself.

"You wanted to lie to her some more?" I asked.

He had a point though, we could have kept the truth from her. You know what they say, what you don't know can't hurt you. If none of us ever told her, she'd be none the wiser, but keeping a secret like that would eat away at me. I wasn't the kind of guy who liked to have shit like that hanging over my head. Not telling her what we were up to was difficult enough. I'd almost blurted it out a handful of times, especially when I was telling her I was about to cum inside her. I wanted to tell her I was trying to get her pregnant. But I hadn't and now here we were.

He looked over at me. "No, but things would have gone differently if we did that. We would have said we're happy and we'll stick by her no matter what. She'd been here right now. With us. She'd never have to know what we did."

"She'd never have to know if we hadn't done it," I pointed out. "We could have skipped right to asking her to stop taking birth control. Who knows, maybe she would have done it."

I doubted it. She seemed adamant that the time wasn't right yet. Fuck only knows what it would have taken to be the right time. That was something we'd never know now. It was also something I wasn't going to dwell on. Life hadn't gone in that direction, there was no point wondering what might have been.

"All of this speculation is getting us nowhere," Oliver snapped. "We did what we did and now we have to wait for her to calm down and deal with it. And she will. She knows the full truth. She'll realise we did it because we love her. Because she belongs to us and we couldn't wait for the future we all want."

"That's ironic coming from the guy who's holding back on the future she wants," I said. "Keeping her a dirty little secret from the world. How do you think that makes her feel?"

"I know how it makes her feel," he growled. "You think I want that for us?"

"Frankly, yes," I said. "I think you love being in control. If you want to hold every single one of the cards in your fist. You decide when the world knows you have a relationship. You decide when she has babies. What else do you decide? What she wears? Who she talks to? What she eats?"

Oliver's expression was steely. "I never wanted to keep her a secret. By the time we were ready to tell everyone, Cat was pregnant. She was still emotionally fragile. It was a risk I couldn't take. It had nothing to do with Marley."

"It had everything to do with Marley," I said. "It's been tearing her apart, having to sneak around. That's not who she is. It's not who she wants to be. You think you can put a bridle on her and tame her, but you can't. Not completely. She's independent. She's not gonna let you put her in a cage and throw away the key. You're her boss at work, but not in life. In life, she's the one who's in charge. And we, all three of us, took a big chunk away from her." I gestured around to all of us.

Oliver snorted. "You were quick enough to agree to this plan. You know why? Because your ego wanted this. Look past the bullshit and see the reality. You're happy she's pregnant. You're happy she didn't get to decide; we did that for her. That we had so much control over her body that she's now carrying a baby that one of us put there."

He lifted his chin and stared me down. "Admit you get off on that. I know I do."

I wanted to deny it, but I couldn't. As fucked up as it was, my cock throbbed. Yeah, I liked having that power over her. But I hated that she was hurting.

"We need to make this right," I said finally. "I'm not going to lose her because of what we did."

"What if we deserve to lose her?" Cole asked. "Maybe she's better off without us."

"You really think that?" I glanced over at him.

He hadn't stopped looking uncertain, but he looked more so now. "I don't know. I feel like… I wanted this, but doesn't that make me as bad as my father? What he did was because he wanted control over my family. Is this any different?"

"We didn't lay a hand on her in a way she didn't like," I said. But still, she said she felt violated. Maybe on some level we were as bad as Cole's father.

"The difference is, we didn't do it to hurt her," Oliver said. "The opposite. In the end, she's going to have a beautiful baby to love. All of this will be completely worthwhile."

"It better be," I said. "If it isn't, we're going to be totally fucked. I'm not sure we aren't already."

"We're not," Oliver said. "Let me ask you a question. If we could do all of this over again, would you? I think both of you would. Because both of you thoroughly enjoyed fucking her and hoping she'd conceive. At least admit that to yourselves."

"I'll never *not* want to fuck Marley," I said.

He was right though. This was exactly what I wanted. I hoped like hell she'd forgive us. I suspected it wouldn't be that easy. It was going to take something fucking spectacular to make it up to her. Something that was going to take time and a butt load of effort.

CHAPTER 22
MARLEY

I had no idea where I was going, I just drove. When I almost ran over a family of ducks, I knew it was time to stop driving.

Somehow, without meaning to, I pulled up the car out the front of Cat's house. I sat in the car and stared for a long time, considering whether I dared to go inside or not. Should I even knock on the door? Maybe I should go home instead. And do what? Tell my parents everything? I wasn't ready to do that. Not yet.

I had no idea what I was ready for, to be honest. Nothing made sense yet. A million things ran through my brain but it was all a jumble. I felt like someone picked up a two thousand piece jigsaw puzzle and threw all the pieces up in the air. They'd landed on the ground and scattered. A few pieces probably got lost forever, meaning the puzzle could never be made again. That hole was right where my heart used to be. Right before I found out the guys I thought I cared about betrayed me. Used me.

Without thinking about it further, I pulled the keys out of the ignition, grabbed my bag and headed up to the front door of Cat's huge house. My parents' house would have fit into this place four or five times over. With three active boyfriends, she needed all the space she could get.

I licked my lips and raised my hand to tap on the door.

I froze. This was a bad idea. I shouldn't be here or anywhere near her. I should get back into my car and drive to… Anywhere but here.

I lowered my hand. I desperately needed someone to talk to, but it couldn't be her. I should go to Eden. Maybe she'd understand.

I started to turn away when the door opened.

"Marley, what are you doing out here?" Cat asked. "Have you been crying? What the hell happened?" She grabbed my arm and all but pulled me inside.

"I shouldn't—" I turned back away from the door, but her hand stopped me from moving further.

"Of course you should," she said. "Come on, let's sit down."

She led me through the entryway and into a cosy lounge room off to the side. She lowered me onto the couch and sat beside me.

"You don't have to tell me anything you don't want to," she said. "But you're obviously upset and need to talk to someone. You know I'm here for you, no matter what, right?"

"Yeah." She might not be there for me when she heard what I had to say. If I could get the words out. "You might not believe what happened."

"I've seen some crazy things," she said dryly. "There's not much I wouldn't believe. Was it Cole and Toby? What did they do? Do I have to go and break some balls? Because I will. Whatever it takes. No one fucks with my friends." She did her best, scary, protective face, which was adorable. Especially as pregnant as she was.

I exhaled slowly and massaged my forehead with my thumb and fingers.

"You could say it's them," I said. I paused for a few beats before saying, "I'm pregnant."

She squealed with joy and threw her arms around me to give me a squeeze. "Congratulations. We're both having babies. This is amazing."

I squeezed her back, but with none of the enthusiasm she displayed.

Finally she peeled herself away and looked at me. "You're not happy about it?"

"I'm not… I haven't had time to think about how I feel about it," I said. "It's how it happened. It's thrown me for a loop." Several loops.

"I'm not the most worldly person in the world, but I have a fair idea of how it happened," she said. "My father made sure I understood all about sex. He insisted he didn't want any accidents because I didn't know what was going on."

I tried not to wince. Oliver Ryan was a fucking hypocrite.

"I know where babies come from," I said. "I was on birth control."

"That's not one hundred percent effective," Cat said. She'd put a lid on her enthusiasm, swapping it out for sympathy.

"I know it's not, if it's actually used," I said with shades of bitterness colouring my tone.

"You… I'm confused." She frowned at me. "You were on birth control, but you weren't using it?"

I sucked in a breath. "I was on what I thought was birth control. I was taking it carefully."

She sat back and placed her hands on her very pregnant belly. "Okay. You thought it was birth control. What was it?"

"Sugar pills," I said. "My birth control was switched for those."

She blinked a couple of times. "Switched? You didn't…"

"No," said quickly. "I didn't change them myself. I wasn't ready. I'm still not sure I am." The more I talked about it, the more bizarre all of this sounded, the more it all hurt.

"If you didn't do it, then who did?" she asked. "If the pharmacy changed them without your knowledge, you can sue their asses. Who does something like that? I always thought we could trust them."

"We can," I said quickly. "It wasn't them." I shook my head. "It was a plan by my boyfriends. They decided to change my pills and get me pregnant on purpose."

Cat's mouth dropped open. She gaped at me for a solid minute. Shook her head.

"Come again? Your boyfriends tampered with your birth control so they could get you pregnant without you knowing or agreeing to it?" She looked completely disbelieving. Not that I was lying, but that she couldn't get her head around what they did.

"I know it sounds crazy," I said. "When I told them I was pregnant, they admitted what they did. They seemed pleased with themselves." Tears trickled down my cheeks again. "They did this to me on purpose and they were happy about it. I feel like I have no idea who any of them are, not at all."

"I think I will break some balls," Cat growled. "How dare they do that to you? I thought what Cruz and Easton did was bad enough, but it was nothing compared to this. Not even fucking close. You must feel so…"

"Angry? Violated? Devastated? All of those things." I leaned against the back of the couch and closed my eyes for a moment. "I have no idea what to think or what to do. What do I even tell the baby when it's born? Hey, I love you but you were put there without my consent. Because three men thought they knew better." I didn't realise what I was saying until the words were out. Once they were, I couldn't take them back, especially when Cat realised.

She frowned. "Three men? Toby, Cole, and?"

Fuck.

I thought quickly, but I'd said too much already. It was too late to correct myself, she probably saw the panic on my face that threatened to overwhelm me.

I whispered, "Toby, Cole and… Your father, Oliver."

She stared at me. "My— No. You wouldn't do that. Not with my father. You're my best friend. There's no way. You can't have."

"I did." I wiped tears off my cheeks. "He and I have been seeing each other."

She shook her head. "How long? How long have you been sleeping with my father?"

I swallowed hard. "About a year. I wanted to tell you but…" Every excuse seemed meaningless now. She was looking at me like I must have looked at the guys, like she didn't know me at all.

"About a year?" she echoed. "Even though you knew how I felt about the very idea of you or Eden being involved with him. Did you even care what I thought?"

"Of course I did," I said, my voice high. "We fell in love with each other. We wanted to be together. He was the one who changed out my pills and hatched the plan with Toby and Cole. It was his idea."

She stared down at my belly. "You might be carrying my brother or sister." She looked slightly green.

"I might be," I admitted. "But I didn't—"

"I don't care what you didn't," she said coldly. "I thought we were friends. Clearly I was wrong. You slept with my father, even knowing how upset I'd be about it. Did you really think you could have a relationship with him? Be my stepmother or something? You're the same age as me, Marley. I've known you almost all my life. So. Has. He. Do you realise how sick that sounds?"

Her eyes were glazed, face pink with anger and disappointment. She looked as though I'd stabbed her in the back and then twisted the knife as hard as I could. The expression on her face was a blade straight to my own heart.

"We never wanted to hurt you," I said. "What we had, I thought it was real. He said he loved me. He wanted to be with me. We were going to tell you after your baby was born. I'm so sorry. Nothing was meant to happen like this."

She looked disgusted. "You work with him. Neither of you had any business touching each other. I trusted both of you to respect my feelings on this. But you didn't. Instead you're here, throwing it in my face."

"That's not what I'm doing," I argued.

My whole world was falling down around my ears. There was nothing I could do to stop it from toppling like a house of cards. "I just needed to talk to someone." All I did was make everything a thousand times worse.

"Cat. What's going on?" Shaw stepped into the

room, his face a mask of worry. He barely gave me a glance, his gaze was all for her. His posture was immediately protective and ready. If she needed anything, he'd do it in an instant. He saved her life once, he'd do it a million times again if he had to.

"I didn't mean to upset her," I said. That was the last thing I wanted. I shouldn't have come here in the first place. I should have stayed far away. I knew she'd be angry when she found out, but I hadn't expected to see that expression on her face. Like she'd be happy if she never saw me again.

"You clearly have," Shaw said coolly. "You should go. Cat, you should get some rest."

He looked as though he'd carry her to bed himself if she tried to argue. He was intense, but his love for her was clear for anyone to see. He wouldn't hesitate to throw himself in front of a bullet for her. A friend who was upsetting her was a small matter in comparison.

I looked over to Cat, silently begging her to try to understand. To tell me to stay so we could talk and work it out. We'd been so close for so long, surely she'd understand deep down.

"You should go," Cat said softly.

With help from her boyfriend, she stood. Before she walked away she said, "I'd like to wish you the best with your baby, but I can't. You made the bed a long time ago, you can lie in it." She slipped out of the room.

Shaw gave me a long, unreadable look. He'd always been protective of her, it didn't surprise me he'd step in when she was getting worked up. I thought my guys would have done the same thing but I was so very fucking wrong.

I'd never seen her so angry. I certainly never thought she'd say something like that to me. Her words cut me deeper than anything the guys could have done, sharper than a scalpel right to my heart. My whole life was shattered into a million pieces. I couldn't even begin to figure out how to start picking them back up and putting them back together.

My legs trembling, I stood and slipped back out the door and into the front seat of my car. Where did I go? What the hell was I supposed to do? I had no idea.

I'd never felt as alone as I did right then.

CHAPTER 23

MARLEY

Eden was waiting for me outside my house when I got home. She was leaning against the side of her car, looking worried. The moment I turned off the engine and got out of my car, she was right there beside me.

"Marley," she said softly.

"Do you hate me too?" I whispered.

"I could never hate you." She drew me in for a hug. "Do you want to tell me what's going on? Shaw rang and said you might need a friend. Something about you being involved with Oliver Ryan?"

"Shaw did that?" We always got along okay, but there was no question of whose side he was on and if he needed to choose, he'd always choose Cat over anyone else. What must that feel like? To have someone pick you over anyone and anything else?

"It was the briefest conversation I've ever had in my

life, but yes." She took my hand and pulled me away from the front of the house. "He seemed concerned."

I sighed and followed her across the street to a small park. We sat down side-by-side on a bench and I buried my face in my hands. I seemed to be doing that a lot today.

When I finally managed to compose myself, I told her everything. What the guys did and Cat's response to me telling her about my relationship with her father.

Eden listened in silence, her hand over mine.

"So you see, I dug myself a hole," I concluded. "I might as well pull the dirt over myself and stay there."

"Sweetie, none of it's your fault," Eden said. "You can't help who you fell for."

She averted her eyes for a moment before looking back at me. "You certainly can't help what those guys did to you. I can't believe any of them would do something so…icky. Tampering with your birth control. I've heard of women deciding not to take theirs so they could get pregnant, but nothing like this. It's worse than poking holes in a condom."

"I can't believe it either," I said. "Part of me wonders if I deserve to have them do that. I lied to Cat and I lied to you. Maybe I'm a shitty person who doesn't deserve anything good."

She put an arm around me and squeezed. "You're one of the sweetest people I know. I won't lie, I'm a bit disappointed you didn't think you could confide in me. But I can't say I'm surprised. I've always thought there was chemistry between you and Oliver. It was only a matter of time before you acted on it. You weren't breaking any laws or rules by caring for each other."

"Tell Cat that," I said bitterly. "She said she didn't want any of her friends to get involved with her father. I didn't listen."

"I love her to pieces," Eden said, "but Cat doesn't get to make the rules. Especially when it comes to your love life or her father's. You would never tell her who she could or couldn't see. She's an adult who made up her own mind, and so are you."

"Maybe she didn't want us getting involved with him because she knew what he was like," I said. "She might have suspected he'd do something like this."

"If she did, I suspect she'd kick him in the balls, not just warn us off him. She'd tell us if she had a clue that he might pull a trick like this. I think it was about her being uncomfortable with the idea of her father being involved with one of her friends, but that's her problem. She'll get over it."

"I don't know about that," I said. "I don't suppose it matters anymore anyway. If he was here in front of me, I'd kick him in the balls myself. He and I are over. Same with Toby and Cole."

"Are you sure about that?" Eden asked carefully. "I mean, I'm not condoning what they did, but maybe there's some way they can make it up to you."

I snorted softly. "I doubt that. I don't think there's anything any of them can do that would make me forgive them. I don't even want to look at any of them right now."

My heart was aching too badly. So much I was convinced it would hurt like this forever. How could it not? How could an ache like this ever ease?

"I understand," Eden said. "This must all be raw. What do you want to do? If you want to get out of town for a while, I'll come with you. Things at home have become a bit strained."

I immediately felt like shit for not asking how she was. She was always so calm and rational. It was easy to assume nothing bad ever happened in her life.

"Is there a problem at home?" I asked.

"My mum and my stepdad are getting a divorce," she said. "When I left, they were arguing over who was moving out. Things were getting…heated."

It was my turn to give her a squeeze. "I'm so sorry, I had no idea."

"It's okay," she said. "It's been going on for a while but recently things have been getting worse. They're really over each other and ready to move on." She looked down at the grass in front of us.

"Are you okay?" I asked. She looked beaten up about it.

"I will be," she said. "But it'll be good to get away for a little while. Let's go lie on a beach somewhere and get some perspective."

"That's so tempting," I said.

"You don't have to go to work tomorrow," she

pointed out. "Looking for a new job can wait for a few days, can't it?"

Normally, I'd say no, but under the circumstances she was right. A few days away wouldn't hurt me and if it gave her a break from the tension at home, then that was a bonus.

"Okay, let's go somewhere. It'll be nice to get away from Opal Springs for a few days." I might even forget what the guys did, for an hour or two.

"Perfect. I have a friend who has a holiday house. I'm sure they won't mind us using it for a few days. I'll get everything organised. Throw a few things into your suitcase and I'll pick you up in an hour."

"Okay, let's do this," I said. If I wasn't careful, I'd let myself get excited.

I was waiting for Eden when she returned, suitcase packed full as though I was going for a year. I sent a text to my parents to let them know I was going away for a few days and ignored three calls from Toby, two from Cole and one from an unknown number that was probably a scam trying to tell me my computer needed an upgrade.

Eden pulled into the driveway, but she was followed close behind by a dark SUV I recognised as Oliver's.

I watched through the window in the door as they both got out of their cars.

Eden stood, hands on fists as Oliver approached. I couldn't hear what they were saying, but they were both just this side of polite, judging by the expressions on their faces. Oliver made to step around her toward the door, but she stopped him with a hand on his chest.

He gave her a look like he'd shove her out of the way if she didn't move. Not usually given to violence, he was obviously short on patience right now.

Before he did anything we'd all regret, I unlocked the door and hurried outside.

"Go away, Oliver," I told him. "I have nothing to say to you."

"You're going somewhere." He frowned at my suitcase, which stood just inside the door.

"It's none of your business," I said. "I can do what I want and go wherever I want. I don't need your permission. I don't belong to you."

He glanced at Eden. "Give us a couple of minutes."

Her eyebrows rose. She looked questioningly at me.

"This won't take long," I told her. Told them *both*. I wasn't giving him a moment more of my time than necessary.

She nodded quickly and stepped a few metres away to give us some space.

Oliver grabbed my arm and pulled me in the opposite direction. "You need to listen to me, Marley-Jane. I know you're angry right now, but you need to calm down and think rationally."

"You need to stop telling me how to think or feel," I snapped. "You don't get to do that anymore."

I won't lie, I was as conflicted as hell. Part of me wanted to hear him out. Maybe he had some explanation that would magically make all of this better. The other part of me didn't want to hear a word.

His grip on my arm tightened. "I can and will tell you. You might not believe it right now, but you do belong to me. You will come to understand why I did what I did. More than that, you'll appreciate it."

I looked him right in the eyes. "In your fucking dreams. You really think I'll understand why you thought it was okay to do what you did? What the hell is wrong with you?"

"Nothing is wrong with me," he said. "Nothing except my desire to give you everything you want and need."

"Whether I like it or not?" I snarled. I shook my head. "That's not how love works."

He barked a laugh. "That's exactly how love works. When you have this baby, you'll understand the lengths people will go to. You'll do anything to make them happy."

"Right now, I think the best thing I can do is keep this baby away from you," I said. "I don't give a shit whether you're the father or not."

"I don't either," he said. He lifted his chin and looked at me from beneath his eyebrows. He looked tired, but I couldn't bring myself to give a shit right now.

"I love you. I'll love this baby, whether or not it's mine. Statistically, there's a greater chance Toby or Cole are the biological father, given they're younger. So is their sperm."

"Thank fuck for that," I said. "Cat hates me enough right now without me carrying her sibling." When I saw I'd had him at a loss for words, I added, "I told her everything. All about us and what you did. She's furious."

His grip tightened harder still, his fingers digging into my flesh. "She wasn't supposed to know until after her baby is born."

"Yeah, well, now she does," I said. "Don't worry, I'm sure she hates you as much as she hates me."

He dropped his hand from my arm. "Fuck."

"Yeah, fuck. I don't suppose it crossed your mind there might be consequences to what you did." I stepped back from him.

He scrubbed a hand over his face. "I should talk to her."

"That's up to you." I shrugged. "If you don't get your car out of my driveway, I'm calling a tow truck to get it removed."

"Marley-Jane." For a moment he actually looked regretful. "How long are you going away?"

"As long as I want," I said. "It's none of your business anymore."

I turned away and looked back up the driveway to

get my suitcase. By the time I turned back, he and his car were gone.

CHAPTER 24

MARLEY

It wasn't until we were about to board our plane that I saw Cole. He carried a long duffel bag over his shoulder and regret on his face.

He looked at me, but didn't say anything or try to approach as we made our way to the boarding gate.

"I'm going to guess his presence isn't a coincidence," Eden remarked. "For the record, I didn't tell him when we were going."

"Neither did I," I said. I gave him a warning look before turning away and following the rest of the passengers onto the plane.

"Is he on the same flight?" I didn't want to look back.

"It looks like it," she said. "I get the distinct impression he's not going to listen if you tell him to go away."

I sighed. "Short of trying to convince the airline he shouldn't be here, I guess there's nothing we can do about it."

I'd have to ignore him and pretend I had no idea who he was. Having him so close, yet so far made my heart hurt. Of all three of the guys, he seemed the least convinced that what they did to me was a good idea. Did that mean I'd forgive him? Fuck no. He admitted to being as much a part of it as the others were.

When he took me from my room, out into the bush, he knew what he was doing. When he tore off my clothes and rammed into me, he knew there was a chance he'd get me pregnant. Did he get off on it? Did that add to his enjoyment? His feeling of control?

My stomach turned and I had to swallow to keep from being sick.

"I'll do what I can to make sure he stays away from you," Eden said. "If nothing else, we can lose him when we get to Queensland. It's a big place, we should be able to lose ourselves."

"Right now, I'm feeling lost enough as it is," I said.

She put her arm around me and gave me a sideways hug before we had to step into the plane single file.

I let her go first, in case I needed to hurry to the toilet. Just as I was getting settled into my seat and adjusting the seat belt, Cole slipped into the seat behind us. He gave me a tentative look on the way past and a faint but apologetic smile.

I responded with a cold stare before I looked away. I reminded myself what he did and that I shouldn't let my guard down for a moment. I couldn't let him get to me. He betrayed my trust and used me. He and the others treated me like I was a piece of meat.

Where did Oliver get off saying I belonged to them? He was fucking delusional.

"We could ask to switch seats?" Eden suggested.

I considered for a moment before shaking my head. "It's nothing I can't handle. I'm going to ignore him and enjoy the flight."

And hope like hell he didn't try anything mid-flight. All the other passengers on the plane would be pissed off if he caused a scene and the plane had to be turned back around to Opal Springs.

In spite of that, I turned back and peered through the gap in the seats. Cole was sitting with his head against the backrest, eyes closed, earbuds in his ears. As if he knew I was looking, he opened his eyes a crack and looked at me.

I immediately whipped my head around to face the front. I fastened my seatbelt and focused on looking past Eden, out the window as we taxied down the runway and took off.

"We should have done this a long time ago," Eden said. "Just jump on a plane and go."

"Will your shop be okay?" I should have thought of that before now, but my brain was preoccupied by too much other shit.

They should just hand the Worst Friend of the Year award to me and be done with it.

"My assistant will cover for me," she said. "It's a

quiet time of year anyway. Not too many weddings or anything like that. The perfect time of year to slip away for a break with one of the best people I know."

"Instead, you're stuck with me," I said bitterly.

She laughed and bumped her shoulder against mine. "I meant you, silly. You're one of the kindest, sweetest people I've ever met." She raised her finger at me. "Don't tell me I need to get out more."

"I mean, if the hat fits." I swatted her hand away. "I know you're trying to be sweet, I just feel crappy right now. When I woke up this morning, everything was fine. There was room for improvement, but I was more or less happy. Now I feel like everything has been tipped upside down."

I resisted the urge to look back at Cole again. If he had no music coming through his earbuds, he could hear what we were saying. Nothing he didn't already know or deserve to hear.

"It'll get easier," she said. "We can spend the next few days having fun and taking your mind off everything. I have a few ideas for things we can do."

"It sucks that none of those things can include getting drunk," I said sourly. That was a surefire way to forget my troubles for a few hours. My baby was going to have a rough enough start in life without me doing that to them.

"We can have fun without drinking," she said. "Trust me."

I winced, then immediately regretted doing that. "I know I can trust you," I said quickly. "I just…"

"You've had your trust betrayed," she said loudly, her face tilted in Cole's direction. "It's totally normal to feel on edge for a while. Whatever happens, I've got your back. Even if I have to kick a few balls for you." She tucked some of her purple hair behind her ear and grinned.

"You're the best," I said. "What about you and Cat? I don't want to get between you."

"You won't," Eden assured me. "I can be there for both of you and not take sides. I've had some practice at that lately."

"Your mother and stepfather?" I guessed.

"Yeah." She scratched a spot right above her eyebrow. "They were only together for a handful of years, but Brock and I got on so well. We're more like friends than father and daughter. He never tried to tell me what to do or anything like that. We used to hang out and drink beer and watch hockey or football. When things started to go bad between them, Mum wanted me to take her side in everything. Brock kept telling her to stop trying to put me in a difficult position. In the end, it was easier not to get in the middle."

"You seemed to enjoy getting in the middle of Mitch and Jagger," I teased lightly.

"That's a middle position I can definitely enjoy," she said. "Those boys know what they're doing with me and with each other."

"I'm happy for you," I said honestly. "They both seem to like you."

"It's nothing serious, but we enjoy spending time together," she said. "Friends with benefits, you know?"

"That sounds perfect," I said. And a lot less complicated than my love life.

"It is," she said. "No offence, but seeing you upset and seeing what my mother is going through, I'm not sure I want it any other way. Love seems like a big hassle."

I leaned back against the headrest and exhaled softly. "Maybe it isn't if you do it right."

"Marley-Jane Hammond," she said sternly. "You didn't do love wrong."

"I just have crappy taste in men?" I suggested.

Once again, I resisted the urge to look back at Cole. Was he a bad person or a good person who made a mistake? I didn't know and I wasn't sure thinking about it for too long was such a good idea right now. Eden was right, I should try to put it all out of my head for a few days and get myself together. Even if I didn't deserve it, the baby did.

"I'm not sure that's the case either," she said. "I don't think any of them are necessarily bad people. They just lack judgement." Again she addressed the remark to Cole as well.

"Maybe, but what else do they lack judgement about?" I asked. "If they could do what they did, what else are they capable of?" If I could bring myself to forgive them, could I trust that they wouldn't fuck up like that again? Maybe they had and I just didn't know.

We were interrupted by the flight attendant rolling her trolley past and offering a snack and something to eat.

Armed with a cup of coffee and a tiny bag of nuts, I peeked back at Cole. He was sitting with a drink of water, his eyes on the gap between the seats. He offered me a faint smile, his eyes full of apology.

I wanted to ask why the hell he was here, on this flight. When we landed, I should tell him to get lost and take the first flight back to Opal Springs. Both of those would require talking to him and I wasn't ready to do that yet. Besides which, I had a feeling if I told him to go home, he'd ignore me. Whatever he was here for, he'd return when he was ready and not before.

"Do you want me to talk to him?" Eden asked. "I don't mind telling him where to go."

I considered for a moment, but shook my head before taking a sip of coffee. "I don't want you in the middle of that either. Not if I can help it."

"I don't mind," she said. "This is different to Mum and Brock or you and Cat. I'm not close to any of those guys."

"You've known Oliver as long as I have," I pointed out. "Yelling at him would cause trouble for you and Cat."

As much as I would enjoy seeing that, it wasn't fair

to ask her to get involved in that way. Besides, knowing him, he'd take every word calmly before eviscerating her with a handful of words. It took a lot to make him angry, but when he did, he was eloquent.

"I'm a big girl," she said. "I can take care of myself."

"So am I," I said. "Kind of." I was going to have to deal with all three of the guys at some point, and I would. With or without Eden.

She grimaced. "When did we become responsible adults?"

I managed a tight laugh. "I'm not sure I'd call us responsible, but I don't know when we became adults. I don't remember agreeing to grow up."

"Neither do I," she agreed. "Let's pretend, for the next few days, that we're kids again. Kids with credit cards."

"That sounds perfect," I said. "Does it have to be pretend? I wouldn't mind going back to being a kid for a while." Everything seemed so much simpler then. My biggest problem was wondering if the fridge would topple over under the weight of all the artwork my mother stuck to it. She assured me that the fridge wasn't going anywhere, but I used to tiptoe past it anyway. When she wasn't looking, I'd peel off older paintings and tucked them away, just in case.

In retrospect, it was pretty dumb, but if I could go back to those days for a bit, I'd do it. They'd have to drag me, kicking and screaming back into adulthood.

"It can be whatever we want it to be," Eden said. "Let's just have some fun."

I raised my coffee. "I'll drink to that." We tapped our paper cups together and laughed.

CHAPTER 25
MARLEY

"Isn't this nice?" Eden sat with her hand raised while the technician painted her nails her favourite colour, purple.

"It's been too long since we did this together." When the technician painting my nails tapped my hand, I slipped it into the dryer and offered her the other one. Mine were a bright, cheerful pink, which helped to elevate my mood somewhat.

"I told you this was a good idea," she said. "This vacation was just what we both needed."

We landed about three hours ago and made our way to our hotel. When we arrived, we were told the accommodation was fully paid up, including an upgrade to a beachfront penthouse.

I wanted to go somewhere else, but Eden convinced me to take advantage of the gift so obviously from Cole.

If it wasn't from him, it was one of the other guys. I shouldn't be surprised they were keeping tabs.

We'd left our suitcases in the hotel and went to explore the sunny Gold Coast. At one point, we passed a group of excited women pulling trolleys along behind them. The trolleys were all stacked high with books. Apparently we arrived at the same time as a reader event was taking place in a nearby hotel.

One of them mentioned Elenna Draeger, one of our favourite authors, but as far as I could tell, tickets were sold out, so Eden and I opted to get our nails done instead.

I was about to say something else when movement near the salon door caught my eye. I looked up to see Cole step inside. He glanced over at me, nodded, then spoke to the woman at the desk. I couldn't hear what they were saying and the conversation only lasted for a minute before he ducked back out again.

"I'm starting to think he's stalking me," I said. That was just what I needed. Not.

"He does seem to appear wherever we are," Eden agreed. She only had a slight frown on her brow. She seemed less concerned that he was following us, than worried he might interrupt our vacation and stress me out.

"Let's try not to think about him," I said. "As long as he leaves us alone, we should be fine. Right?"

"Exactly." Eden nodded. "Maybe he was asking for directions." She didn't look like she believed it either.

"Doesn't everyone have a GPS on their phone these days?" I asked.

"To be honest, I could get lost even with the help of a GPS," she said with a laugh. "He might be the same."

"If he is, it's the mother of all coincidences," I said. No, he was definitely here for a reason. One we discovered when we went to pay for our pedicures and manicures.

"They're already paid for," the woman at the desk said with a smile. "That cute guy who popped in paid for them, for you both. I think he likes you."

"Yeah, maybe," I said. I followed Eden out of the salon and glanced around, looking for Cole. "First the hotel, now this. Is he going to follow us around and pay for everything the whole time we're here?"

"It would seem like it," she said. "I can't decide if that's the sweetest thing I ever heard or the creepiest."

"I'll take all of the above," I said. "I never asked for him to do anything like that."

"Isn't that the point?" She gestured over to an ice cream shop and started walking. "He's trying to do nice things for you."

"If he thinks paying for me to get my nails painted will make up for what he and the others did, he's going to have to think again," I said. I ordered my ice cream and stood back while they made it.

The server placed a scoop of chocolate and a scoop of chocolate mint on a cone and put it in front of me before making Eden's order.

"I'll have the same as her," Cole said, stepping into the shop behind me and pointing to my cone. "I'm paying for these."

I turned to him and gave him my best side eye. "What do you think you're doing?"

He shrugged. "Getting ice cream."

"That wasn't what I was referring to, and you know it," I said. Before I could stop him, he had his phone out, tapping the screen. He took his own cone and stepped back out of the shop.

With a frustrated growl under my breath, I took my cone, smiled at the server and stepped back out to the footpath.

"What Marley wants to know is, are you stalking her?" Eden asked.

Cole licked his ice cream in a way that had me stopping and staring in spite of myself.

I forced myself to look away before he could affect me too much. I reminded myself of what he did and why I was pissed off at him.

"I wouldn't call it stalking," Cole said. "I'm just following around the woman I love and making sure she has everything she needs."

"That sounds like stalking to me," I said. "I came here to get away from you, not so you could be there every time I turn around. Do the others know where I am?"

"Not specifically," he said. "They know roughly

where you are and that I'm keeping an eye on you. I told them you're all right, but need some space."

"And yet, here you are," I said. "Not giving me space."

He took a step back.

I rolled my eyes. "Shouldn't you be in training? Kage is going to be pissed off with you." Not that I gave a shit. That was his problem, not mine.

"I told him I had an emergency," Cole said. "I had a family member who needed me. Nothing about that isn't right."

"We're not family," I said.

"You're my family," he said. "Even if you hate my guts, you will be. The way I feel about you, it's not going to go away."

"Apparently, neither are you," I said.

He actually smiled at that. "No, I'm not. Like I said, I'm keeping an eye on you and making sure you're okay."

"I'm not okay," I said. "Not even close. I'm not sure I ever will be. If you wanted me to be okay, you shouldn't have done what you did."

"There aren't words to tell you how sorry I am about that," he said. "But if I have to spend the rest of my life trying to find a way to make it up to you, then that's what I'll do. Fuck playing hockey. This will be my job if that's how it has to be."

"Until you run out of money," I said.

"I'll find a way," he said. "Nothing in my life is as important as this. As you."

"What about Toby?" I asked.

"I care about him too, but you're my first priority at the moment," Cole said. "He can take care of himself."

"Why did you do it?" I asked. "You could have told Oliver no."

"I could have," he agreed. He licked melted ice cream off his fingers.

I tried to ignore the way my clit throbbed at the sight of his tongue.

"Why didn't you?" I asked insistently.

"Because my family is fucked up," he said finally. "I wanted a family that wasn't fucked up, but I went about it in a fucked up way."

"You can say that again," Eden said. "Families aren't a thing that you can force. They happen or they don't. And sometimes they don't work out the way you think they will. Going behind the back of one family member with another is a surefire way to mess everything up."

She seemed to be referring to something specific, but couldn't focus on that just now. I turned back to Cole.

"You're right, you did go about it in a fucked up way," I said. "I don't know if I can ever forgive you, but I appreciate that you didn't try to lay the blame on Oliver or Toby. You could easily have tried to say they convinced you."

"It was Oliver's idea, but I went along with it," Cole said. "I own what I did. And I own what I should have done. I should have talked to you. That's something I'm going to have to live with for the rest of my life." He opened and closed his mouth a couple more times before shaking his head.

"I'm not going to stop looking out for you. But I'll keep my distance for now. If you need anything, you only have to—"

"Look over my shoulder?" I suggested.

He glanced down and back up again. "Something like that." He gave us both a slight nod before slipping away down the street.

"He seemed genuinely sorry," Eden said.

"You think I should forgive him, don't you?" I asked.

"I think you should do whatever is right for you," she said. "If that means forgiving him and moving on, then you should at least consider it. If never seeing him again is best for you, then that's the choice you need to make. But I genuinely think he didn't mean to hurt you. You did want children someday, didn't you? Maybe not now, but some day."

"Definitely not now," I said. "It's not the baby that's the problem, it's them thinking they could control me."

"I think it's safe to say they've learned their lesson there," she said. "I very much doubt they'd pull anything like this ever again."

"If I forgive them, they might," I said. "They might see it as a sign to do whatever they want."

"Judging by the look on Cole's face, he'd stop them

before they did anything stupid." She bit into her ice cream cone.

He might, but that was no guarantee. They'd broken my trust. It would take a lot more than nail polish and ice cream to patch that up. I had no idea what it would take, but more than that at least.

"Do you think he was serious that he'd give up hockey for me?" I asked. "Just so he could keep trying to make things right?"

He seemed adamant that's what he would do, but hockey was his life. Something he'd worked for since he was a kid. To even think about giving that up for me, was huge. Bigger than huge. What would he do with himself if he wasn't on the ice, defending the goal against aggressive opposition players? Being my shadow would get old pretty quickly, wouldn't it? I'd get bored if I was following myself around.

"If I was him, I'd give it up in a heartbeat," Eden said. "I can see how much he loves you. You're more important to him than slapping around a puck with a stick."

"Maybe," I said uncertainly. "I think I'm going to need a nice, long swim to work off all of this ice cream." That might help take my mind of him for a while. One of the best things about the Gold Coast was being able to shop in the morning, swim in the afternoon and eat in a fine restaurant at night.

"I was going to suggest that," she said. "A good, long

swim followed by a massage, then dinner. Somewhere really expensive."

"Is this where you tell me not to forgive him too soon, so we can enjoy a five-star holiday at his expense?" I asked dryly.

"I hadn't thought of that, but now you mention it, you have a point," she said. "Why shouldn't we enjoy ourselves as much as we can? I haven't had lobster in years." She grinned and wiped her fingers on her napkin.

I didn't know if I wanted to take advantage of him that way, but lobster did sound good.

CHAPTER 26
MARLEY

"Hey beautiful, you're looking lonely over here." Slicked back blonde hair, brown eyes and a T-shirt that proudly proclaimed him as a fan of some football team, he slid into the stool beside me. "I thought I'd keep you company."

"I'm fine, thanks," I said dismissively. I gave him no more than a glance before looking away.

"Don't be like that," he said. "We both know how this is going to go down. I buy you a couple of drinks, you and I go back to my hotel room and you use that pretty little mouth on my cock. Everyone has a good time. If you have a husband at home, don't worry, I won't tell him." He lifted his beer glass to his mouth and grinned.

I saw the wedding ring around his finger and felt sorry for his wife.

"Like I said, I'm fine, thanks," I said.

I looked toward the toilets, but saw no sign of Eden

returning. Usually, we'd go together, but I was holding our seats and watching over our drinks. A girl could never be too careful, no matter where she went.

"Yes, you are." He looked me up and down. "I'm Jarrod, and you are..." He raised an eyebrow expectantly.

"Not interested," I said. "Go and find someone else to cheat on your wife with. Or better yet, don't cheat at all. I mean, you wouldn't want to take home some kind of nasty disease." I hoped that would deter him, but he just grinned.

"Don't be like that. You know you want it. Girls like you always do."

"Girls like me?" I turned around slightly to face him. "You don't look like you have a lot of experience with girls like me."

"Maybe I don't," he shrugged. "This could be the perfect opportunity to change that. Wouldn't you say?" He actually winked at me. Winked.

I couldn't tell if the turning in my stomach was morning sickness or this dickhead. Maybe both.

"No, I wouldn't say that," I said. "Like I said, I'm not interested. If you don't want to leave, I'll call security."

He sneered at me and slipped down off the stool. He stalked away muttering something like, "Would have been a bad fuck anyway."

He was barely gone when Eden finally returned.

"Don't leave me alone again," I said, eyes wide. I told her about Jarrod and we both had a good laugh.

"I don't dare leave you alone again," she said, still giggling. "Although, he sounds like an absolute catch."

"I'm sure he's an absolute *something*," I said. "I don't know about a catch. I'd be more likely to catch something if I went with him."

Eden burst out laughing again. "At least you know you've still got it."

"If it attracts guys like that, I'm not sure if I want it," I said.

I drank what was left of my juice and tried to stifle a yawn. "I don't know about you, but I'm about ready to wrap this up for the night." It wasn't much before midnight anyway.

"Me too," Eden nodded. She downed the last of her beer and set the glass on the bar. "Let's go."

It wasn't until we stepped back out onto the street that I realised we were being followed. By more than one person, and neither of them was Cole.

"We figured we'd give you the chance to change your mind," Jarrod said. "Nice of you to bring a friend." He was with a man who looked enough like him to have been his brother. If you turned the sleaze-o-metre up to double.

Eden snorted. "In your dreams."

"See," Jarrod said slowly. "I'm pretty easy-going, but Zaden here doesn't like to take no for an answer." He gestured towards his brother.

Zaden grunted. "You were right, they'd both look good on their knees."

There were people around, even at this time of night, but no one seemed to be paying any attention. No one but us saw Zaden pull out a small blade.

He fixed a stone cold look on Eden. "Get on your knees, bitch."

For the first time, I was actually scared. He looked as though he wouldn't hesitate to use the knife on one of us if we didn't do exactly what they said.

Zaden growled. "I said, get on your knees."

Apparently he didn't count on a tall, muscular professional hockey player coming barrelling out of the bar behind him and throwing himself on Zaden.

They both fell heavily to the ground. The blade slipped out of Zaden's fingers and skittered across the concrete.

Jarrod made a lunge for it, but Eden was quicker. She grabbed it up, closed the blade and curled her fingers around it.

Jarrod sneered, but instead of going after her, he gripped the back of Cole's shirt and tried to pull him off his brother.

At the same time, Zaden tried to shove the weight off his back.

"Get the fuck of me," he snarled. "I'll call the fucking cops."

Cole shook off Jarrod and rolled off Zaden, but he didn't let him go. Instead, he dragged him to his knees and planted his fist in the other man's face.

Both Jarrod and Zaden swore. Blood poured down Zaden's face.

Jarrod tried again to grab Cole and punch him in the face, but Cole was too fast for him. He got to his feet, knocked Jarrod's legs out from under him and dropped him to the ground.

"You're fucking nuts," Zaden growled. His hand was pressed to his nose. "Jarrod, let's get the fuck out of here."

Groaning, Jarrod rolled over and pushed himself to his feet. He looked at Cole like he might try again to take a swing, but in the end he shook his head and staggered away after his brother.

Cole watched them go, shaking out the pain in his already red hand.

"That's going to need some ice," I said.

He glanced down at it vaguely and nodded. "Yeah, I guess. Are you two okay?"

"Thanks to you we are," Eden said. "That was…" Her eyes were wide, staring.

I wrapped my arms around her and rubbed my hand up and down her back. I whispered reassuring words in her ear until she stopped shaking. She clung to me for a few minutes before regaining her composure.

"Thank you," I said to Cole. "If you weren't here…"

"You would have figured out something," he said. "I just saw them follow you and when I saw that knife, I lost my mind. If anything happened to you…" He shook his head.

"Nothing did, because of my benevolent stalker." Apparently I dealt with situations like this with dark humour. I reached out my hand and pulled him to me, in an awkward, three-way hug. Somehow my lips found my way to his.

He might have faith that we would have found a way out of the situation, but I didn't. If it wasn't for him, those assholes could have forced themselves on both of us. Or worse.

Zaden might have killed Eden or me, or my baby. For the first time since I found that I was pregnant, I was truly protective of this life growing inside me. Right now, I couldn't bring myself to care how their existence came about. I was just grateful to be alive.

Cole kissed me gently, but mostly he held me while I held Eden.

"We should get out of here," I said after I didn't know how long. Maybe a few minutes, maybe half an hour. Fear and fatigue muddled my brain.

"Here, outside this bar, or here, the Gold Coast?" Eden asked.

"The first, and then the second. I'm ready to go home," I said.

I looked up at Cole and managed a smile. My anger towards him seemed to have cooled slightly. I hadn't forgiven him, but maybe in time, I could.

Whether I could forgive Toby or Oliver was another story.

Cole must have noticed, because he whispered, "I

know it won't be easy. I wish it took something other than this for you to see how much I care about you."

I leaned back and looked around both ways. When he gave me a funny look I said, "I was checking to see if Oliver was around. Just in case he set that up."

"If he did, I'm going to break his face too," Cole said. "I didn't tell either of them you were here tonight. For what it's worth though, they're both worried about you."

"Are you going to tell them what happened?" I asked.

"I think they should know," Cole said. "What we did led to this moment. This was our fault as much as it was those asshole's."

"You didn't ask them to pull a knife on us," I said. I rested the side of my head against his chest. He felt warm and solid. I didn't realise how much I needed this until right now. I'd missed him more than I'd expected to. Touching him now felt real and right. I never thought I'd feel this way again, but it felt good. Letting go of some of my anger was a relief.

"We might as well have," he said. "If it wasn't for us, you wouldn't be anywhere near here right now."

"If it wasn't us, they might have tried to attack some other women who didn't have a big, bad ass hockey player to defend them," I said.

Eden and I might have been able to fend off the potential attackers, but not without getting hurt in the process. I'd always be grateful to Cole for stepping in when he did.

"That's right," Eden said. "Another woman might not have been so lucky. Hopefully they think again before they try anything like that." She shuddered.

Tonight would likely haunt her nightmares for a while. Mine too. Even now, the stone cold expression in Zaden's eyes made my stomach twist. He would have done what he tried to do without a second thought. I hoped his nose was very, very broken. And extremely painful.

"I have some friends in the police," Cole said. "I'll let them know what happened. There's probably cameras around here somewhere. They'll deal with those assholes." He slipped the knife out of Eden's hand and tucked it into his pocket. "Let's get you back to your hotel room. I'll book us on the first flight out in the morning."

"Thank you," I said again, before lightly kissing his mouth. "I'm glad you were stalking me."

He snorted softly. "I'm glad I was too. I think I'll keep doing it."

"I think you should stick to playing hockey," I told him.

"You're going to need it when your credit card bill comes in," Eden said. She gave him her best innocent-but-not-really-innocent smile. We hadn't taken advantage as much as we could have, but he wouldn't know that until he checked his account. Why not let him sweat for a while? Not too long, just enough to make up for the past. He'd be the first to suggest it was deserved.

That drew a smile from him. "I don't doubt it. I also have no regrets about that. I know how much fun both of you had up until tonight. I've enjoyed watching it. Any time you want to do it again, let me know."

"You might not regret it now, but you might come to regret saying that eventually," I said with a grin. "When we take you up on it."

He raised his hands, his fingers outstretched. "Bring it on. It'll mean you're still talking to me."

"I guess it might," I said. Talking was a start. Anything else—we'd see.

"I'll take it," he said. "Come on, let's go. Before those two come back with a bunch of friends. Punching them all out would hurt." He opened and closed his hand a few times. It clearly hurt, but he wasn't going to complain. Hopefully it wouldn't affect his playing too much when we got home. The team deserved better.

The three of us intertwined, we headed back to the hotel.

CHAPTER 27

COLE

"That looks painful," Toby remarked.

I placed the icepack on my hand and suppressed a wince. "Nothing I can't deal with."

The pain was easier to deal with than returning to Opal Springs with a swollen hand and being yelled at by Kage Foster. Even after I told him what happened, he was still unimpressed with me. I got the usual lecture about saving the aggression for the ice. With a small hint that suggested he was actually proud of me for defending Marley and Eden. As if I would have stood by and let them be raped.

Toby leaned his shoulder against his locker and crossed his arms. "So Marley forgave you after you defended her honour? And paid for a shit load of stuff?"

"I don't know if she's forgiven me, but we travelled back together," I said. "She let me drive her back to her place. And we're meeting for lunch."

"I'm coming too," he said, with no hesitation.

"I figured you would," I said. "That was why I told you."

I didn't want to have to choose between Marley and Toby. The sooner they figured their shit out, the better.

Toby clapped me on the shoulder. "You're a good man. I wish I'd thought of stalking her."

"I wasn't stalking her," I said.

I grabbed out a T-shirt and pulled it over my still damp hair. In spite of my hand, Kage insisted I take part in training, even pushing me harder than usual. Apparently he had a sadistic side. I didn't mind. Training hard made me feel more alive than sitting back and watching.

"I was following her around to make sure she was alright. Stalking is something people do when they're fucked up in the head."

I didn't really give a shit what they called it, the fact was, if I hadn't done what I did those guys would have touched her. Seeing them near her made me red with fury. When that prick sat beside Marley and talked to her, I wanted to rip his head off and shove it up his ass. I considered approaching, but from where I sat, a few tables away, she had the situation under control. If she hadn't, I wouldn't have hesitated to deal with him then and there.

"Of course it is," Toby said. "Let me ask you something. How did it feel to punch both of those dickheads? I know you worry about getting violent off the ice."

I should have known he'd understand what was going on inside my brain.

"It felt good," I admitted. "Defending her and her friend felt good. Those pricks weren't innocent, defence-less people. They deserved everything they got. Giving that to them, while she watched… I'd do it again."

"Of course you would," he said. "We'd do anything to take care of her. You, me and Oliver." He turned so his back was against the locker. "What the hell do I do to get her to forgive me? It seems unlikely some other asshole will try to have a go at her."

"No, and you're not asking someone to," I said firmly.

He turned his face and grinned. "I wasn't even thinking that."

I snorted. "Sure you weren't. Don't do it because she will never forgive you and I'll be forced to punch the living shit out of you."

"As if you could," he scoffed. "Don't stress, I wasn't really gonna do anything like that. But, what do I do? I feel like you have a laundry list of grand gestures over me. What have I got? Apart from my good looks, amazing personality and huge cock."

"You could try being yourself?" I suggested. "Apolo-gise for what we did. Grovel if you have to."

"I'm not beneath grovelling, but I've never had to do

shit like that. I don't know where to start." He leaned his head back and closed his eyes.

"Sounds like you need to read more romance books," I said. "When the men in those fuck up, they often have to grovel. Apparently readers swoon over the perfect grovel."

"So, in order to get her to forgive me, I have to become the perfect book boyfriend?" Toby sounded sceptical. "Only, in real life. Wait, you read romance books?"

I shrugged. "They're entertaining. And I like the smut."

"Huh, that figures. I might have to try one. So, any tips for the perfect grovel?" He looked over at me again.

"I've read that some women like it when men beg on their knees," I said.

"Beg on their knees, hmmm? I'm not beneath doing that either. I might try some other stuff first." He frowned. "You think Oliver is coming up with ways to grovel? His grovel game might be better than mine."

"Considering he was the one who tampered with her birth control and came up with this whole plan in the first place, his grovel game is going to have to be first-class," I said. "I feel like it's going to be harder for her to forgive him than us."

"You might be right," Toby said. "But that doesn't mean I get to be a slouch. I am going to lunch with you and her and then I'm coming up with the best grovel you've ever fucking seen."

I clapped him on the shoulder. "I wish you luck, my friend. Let me know if you need any help setting anything up. Or keeping her occupied for a few hours." I wanted to do more than hug and kiss her. I wanted to show her how much she meant to me. And how much the baby growing inside her meant to me.

"I'm sure that would be a hardship," Toby said sarcastically. He sighed out his nose. "They say the course of true love isn't easy. They weren't fucking wrong. Not gonna lie, I'm happy things between you and me are easier." He leaned over to lightly brush his lips over mine.

Our mouths still touching, I laughed softly and said, "Maybe I should have made you grovel."

"You just want me on my knees," he said.

His words made my pulse race and my cock twitch in response. "I wouldn't be adverse to that, but if we don't hurry, we're going to be late for lunch. That will definitely not help your grovel game."

"Hell no it won't," he agreed. "Lunch first, blowjob later. With any luck, we can have a nice little threesome."

"I'd like that," I said.

I'd like that a lot.

No one can say I didn't learn my lesson when it came to keeping things from Marley. I texted her to let her know

Toby would be joining us for lunch. I thought she might respond that he wasn't welcome, but she just sent back **'okay.'**

When we arrived at the coffee shop, her expression was guarded, but not unwelcome. She kissed me, but all Toby got was a brief smile before we took our seats.

"You're looking as beautiful as ever," Toby said, smoothly making sure he was sitting next to her. And that he paid for her lunch.

"Thanks." She sat back in her chair and looked awkward.

"Let me start by saying I'm more sorry than you could ever know," Toby said. "You have to know I'd move heaven and earth to make it up to you."

"Would you?" she asked. She was clearly not planning to make this easy on him. He might end up begging on his knees yet.

"Yeah, I would," he said. "Whatever I have to do, just say the word. You forgave Cole; I'm hoping you can find it in your heart to forgive me too."

"Who says I forgave Cole?" She nodded in my direction. "Did he say that?"

"I think I said you don't hate me as much as you did," I said. "We're working on the rest."

"Hmmm, that sounds about right," she said. She turned back to Toby. "I don't know what to tell you. This isn't about you doing or saying exactly the right thing and magically everything is all right. Cole, doing the things he did, showed he really cared about me."

"I can follow you around, pay for stuff, then punch a couple of guys out," Toby offered.

"That gig is taken." I bit into a corner of my sandwich. "Get your own."

"Thanks," Toby said sarcastically. "Love you too." In spite of his tone, his gaze lingered on mine long enough to make my heart skip a beat. If we could make this work, I'd be the happiest defenceman in the league.

I toasted him with my sandwich and went on eating.

Toby snapped his fingers. "I have an idea. You're going to love it." Instead of elaborating, he picked up his roll and tore off a chunk to put in his mouth.

"Don't go punching people out until I have to forgive you to make you stop," Marley said.

Toby looked like he was about to choke on his mouthful, but swallowed and washed it down with a gulp of coffee. "Why didn't I think of that?" He grinned.

"Because Kage Foster would have your balls turned into pucks?" I suggested.

"Totally worth it," Toby said easily. "Let's call that plan B. Or maybe plan C, because you both like my balls so much." He wriggled his eyebrows like the cocky prick he was.

"Should I be worried he's up to something?" Marley asked me.

"Probably, but for the record, I have no idea what it is," I said. "If it sucks, it's all on him."

"Here lies Toby Glover, thrown under the bus by

someone he thought cared about him," Toby said dramatically.

I chuckled. "No part of it wasn't true, bro. I have no idea what's hatching in that brain of yours." It probably involved orgasms. It was hard not to think about those around Marley. Even harder not to crawl under the table and lick her pussy until she screamed. Or suck Toby's cock until he came down my throat. Maybe one and then the other.

"Something so awesome you'll wish you thought of it," Toby said. "Stalking Marley will pale in comparison to this."

"Please don't do anything stupid," Marley said. "Don't get arrested and kicked off the team. Don't get anyone else arrested either. And don't add to, or subtract from, the population."

"Definitely not on the last count," Toby said. "There's only one person in the world I'm ever having babies with, and that's you. I went about it the wrong way and I suck. I'll prove to you that I'm a good guy. You'll never have another reason to mistrust me ever again."

She looked doubtful, but nodded. "I don't know if you can do that, but I guess I can give you a chance to try." The expression on her face made it very clear that this was a last chance. We fuck up like that again and we were both out on our asses, as they say. Whatever the fuck that meant.

"I won't let you down," Toby promised. He glanced up over my shoulder and frowned.

I turned around to look at what he was staring at. Oliver had stepped into the coffee shop and spotted us. His expression was difficult to read, but he didn't seem angry, not yet. Nor did he look like he was going to get on his knees and beg for Marley's forgiveness. Whatever it was he wanted, he moved through the tables towards us.

"Toby, Cole." He greeted us both with a nod. "Can you give us a moment? I need to talk to Marley."

"Of course you do," Toby drawled. "I have things to do. I'll catch up with you all later."

I waited until Marley nodded that it was okay to leave her alone with Oliver. I picked up what was left of my sandwich and coffee and stepped a few metres away. Close enough to be there for her if she needed me.

CHAPTER 28
MARLEY

I rested my hands in my lap and looked over the table at Oliver. He looked tired. More so than usual. He hadn't shaved in several days, leaving his chin covered in a mess of brown and silver stubble. His hair was slightly longer and messy, as though he hadn't brushed it in a couple of days.

He looked like a different man from the professional, put together Oliver I was used to. Sexier, if I was honest with myself.

I arched one brow and waited for him to speak. No way in fuck was I making this easy on him.

He scrubbed a hand over his face. "I'm sorry you feel the way you do about what I did. My intention wasn't to upset you. The opposite, in fact. I did what I did because I love you. I saw the way you looked at Cat's belly. I saw the longing in your eyes. You said you weren't ready to have a baby, but I think otherwise."

"Obviously," I said simply. "Who gave you the right to make that decision?"

"Me," he said. "I took it upon myself to make that choice. I did what I did with your birth control. I brought Toby and Cole in on everything. They would have been involved either way, but I decided to open the line of communication and let them in."

I made a vague sound in the back of my throat. "But you decided not to let me in. That seems like somewhat of an oversight." That might be the understatement of the year.

He propped his elbows on the table and steepled his fingers. "It wasn't an oversight. I wanted to give you a gift. And I did. How could I regret helping the child growing inside you to exist?"

I leaned forward and propped my own elbows on the table. "Are you listening to yourself? Do you know how fucked up that sounds?"

"I know it's an unorthodox present, but I thought you'd like it better than another bunch of flowers. Anyone can buy you those. They sit in a vase for a few days, then they die. Instead, you get a living gift. One which will bring you so much joy. You're going to be the most amazing mother."

I couldn't decide what was more fucked up, his reasoning or the fact it actually made sense. I must be losing my mind. Now I got used to the idea, I was looking forward to meeting my baby. I didn't care if it was a boy or a girl, I'd teach them how to be the best, most badass versions of themselves they could be. Was what he did so wrong?

Apart from the fact it was illegal.

Regardless of everything, I had no plans to tell the police. Oliver was an incredible, caring doctor and Opal Springs needed him. But there was something I needed to know.

"Have you ever messed with anyone else's medicine?" I asked.

He looked at me directly, his blue eyes intense. "Never. Never before and not again. I'll swear on anything you want."

"What if I forgave you and you decided I wanted another baby?" I asked. "Would you do it again then?"

He hesitated.

"That was what I thought." I adjusted my glasses and shook my head. "You can't go around deciding things like that on behalf of someone else. You wouldn't do something like that to Cat."

"I wouldn't have to," Oliver said. "If they thought she wanted another baby, her boyfriends would deal with it."

I couldn't deny the accuracy of that, but they'd probably talk her into it, not pull tricks like Oliver did.

"Can I ask you something?" I asked.

"Anything," he said earnestly. The heels of his hands pressed together, he spread his fingers apart. "I'm an open book."

He was anything but that, but I decided not to bring that up right now.

"You said you don't regret what you did, but do you really care that this baby might not be yours?" I didn't know why that mattered, but it did.

"In a way I do," he said slowly. "I love the idea of my child growing inside you. But I'm going to love the baby regardless. As long as you're the mother, then I don't care who the father is." He reached over and curled his fingers around mine. "I love you, Marley-Jane. You're the most important person in the world to me. Everything and everyone else is a distant second at best."

"Even—" I started to say.

"So it's true." Cat stopped beside the table and looked down at us. "You are seeing each other."

I pulled my hand from his and sat back. "Not necessarily," I said. "Right now, we're having a conversation. Nothing more than that. You're welcome to join us if you want."

She looked like she might refuse, but Easton strode up behind her and placed a hand on the back of her neck.

"I think it's a good idea," he said. "You don't hold grudges. Why hold one against your father and Marley?"

"What Easton said," I said brightly. "Please." I gestured towards the two empty chairs at the table.

Reluctantly, Cat let Easton pull out a chair and help

her down into it. He sat down beside her, close enough that their shoulders were almost touching. No one would ever doubt his feelings for her. They were good together.

"How are you feeling?" Oliver asked. Always the doctor and father. His expression had softened, like it always did when he spoke to his daughter. No one could doubt his love for her either.

I have to confess, some of my anger towards him melted away. He did what he did out of love, even if it was fucked up.

"Tired," Cat said. "Looking forward to getting this bowling ball out of my stomach." She rested her hands on her round bump.

"You've never been so beautiful," Easton said. He looked at her like he didn't know whether to fuck her or gobble her up. Clearly he liked seeing her so pregnant.

"I've never felt more like a whale," she said. She sighed heavily, but she was absolutely gorgeous. Her red hair was lush and thick, falling to her shoulders in waves.

"Easton is right, you're beautiful," I said. "Glowing."

"Easton is always right," Easton said with a grin.

"So humble too," I teased. "It must be a thing with Opal Springs men. Especially the Ghouls."

"You're not wrong," Cat said. "Try living with three of them." She rolled her eyes, but followed that with an affectionate glance toward Easton.

"Ignore her," Easton said. "She loves every minute of

it." He seemed absolutely certain of that. He'd never been short on confidence, even when he was a carpenter, not a professional winger. He was always certain the Ghouls would turn pro. If they hadn't, he would have signed with a team in another city. He had talent to spare and he knew it.

"Keep telling yourself that," she teased.

He kissed her cheek and got back to his feet. "I'll go and order us some lunch." He disappeared off to the front of the coffee shop.

Cat's gaze lingered on his ass until it was hidden behind a handful of people and tables.

She looked toward me, then to Oliver. "I don't know what to think. Marley told me what you did. I wish I could say I'm surprised. You always did think you knew better than everyone else."

"I'm a father and a doctor, it's my job to know better than anyone else," Oliver said.

He couldn't have looked any more smug if he tried. And there I was, thinking hockey players had big egos. Now I thought about it, they were as bad as each other.

Unfortunately for me, that was part of their attraction. They were confident to the point of arrogance, but they never gave up on what they wanted.

"There's that Opal Springs humility," I said, addressing the comment directly to Cat.

"I noticed that," she said with a smirk and a nod. "I thought things were bad in Melbourne. I think these guys might be a hundred times worse, they just hide it better."

"That sounds accurate," I said. After a moment and a soft sigh, I said, "I'm sorry about everything. We should have told you what was going on from the start. It might have been easier if we had."

She smiled softly and cocked her head a couple of degrees. "Probably not," she said. "It was always going to be weird to think of my father and any of my friends doing…you know."

"Having sex?" Oliver said helpfully.

Cat wrinkled her nose. "Please, never, ever say that again. Give me some time to get used to the idea of you going out on dates and spending time together. The rest of it is nothing I need to know. If there is anything *to* know." She looked back and forth between us again.

"That's up to Marley," Oliver said.

"*Now* you leave something up to me," I said. "I need some time to think about everything. I can't just jump right into forgiving you and trusting you again."

"Will you at least agree to come back and work for me?" He looked pained. "I have a temporary office manager, but she's not you. She doesn't understand the way I like things done."

I only had to hesitate for a few moments before I nodded. I liked my job. Whatever happened between Oliver and I, I enjoyed working in the surgery.

"I might need a pay raise before I can be convinced." I couldn't resist trying.

"It's all yours," he said. "We'll discuss exactly how much later." He looked as though if I insisted on double, he'd agreed to it. Since that would mean the patients had to pay more money, I wouldn't ask for that, but a little bit wouldn't hurt.

"Deal," I said. "I'll start back on Monday morning."

He looked relieved. "Thank you. I've been lost without you." He was clearly referring to more than just the surgery, like he might unravel if I kept him at arm's length much longer.

"Of course you have," I said. "I'm amazing." He was also very particular about the way he liked the surgery run.

When I first started working for him, it took me weeks to figure everything out, so he didn't have to keep rearranging things and watching over everything I did. Eventually, we had the place running like clockwork. I'd gotten good at anticipating all of his needs.

And then there was the fact I hated the idea of another woman working closely with him. Even after everything, I couldn't stop the pang of jealousy and possessiveness that passed through me. He wouldn't cheat, but the idea of another woman seeing him the way I did made me want to scratch her eyes out.

"It isn't just the men of Opal Springs who are humble," Cat teased. "If you ever get sick of working for my father, you can come and work for me. I'm thinking of starting my own surgery after the baby is born."

"Does that mean you don't hate me anymore?" I asked.

"I never hated you," she said. "I'm sorry I was nasty to you. I was just surprised, that was all." She leaned over to give me an awkward hug.

"Hopefully there's no more surprises like that in the works." We both looked at Oliver meaningfully.

He raised his hands. "If there are, I'm not aware of them. Which doesn't mean there aren't."

I shook my head and groaned. "Figures." Hopefully there weren't any more bad surprises at least. I'd had more than enough of those to last a lifetime.

I barely finished that thought when Cole approached the table.

"Toby needs to see us. All three of us."

CHAPTER 29

MARLEY

Cole didn't look worried, but he also didn't look like he knew what Toby needed us for. Taking my cue from him, I decided not to worry too much. Instead, I followed him to his car, Oliver's hand on my lower back. I slipped into the front passenger seat, Oliver in the backseat, behind me.

"Where are we going?" I asked.

Cole slipped into the driver's seat and shrugged. "I only have an address. I'll take us there now." He started the engine and backed the car out of the space.

I looked behind me and shared a smile with Oliver. He was clearly thinking the same thing I was. Remembering Toby catching us out in the car park near the surgery. That led me to remember what we'd almost been caught doing.

The memory of Oliver fucking me in the back of my car made my heart race like crazy. No denying I'd missed him. I'd missed all of them, their hands, their mouths, their cocks.

I turned back around and watched out the window as Opal Springs passed by. We drove from the centre of town out to a more affluent suburb.

Cole pulled up in front of a large house and took out his phone to double check the address. "This is the place."

I exchanged another look with Oliver before removing my seatbelt and climbing out of the car.

I'd just closed the door behind me when Toby stepped out of the front of the house. He spread his arms out wide.

"Welcome," he said with a grin. "I was hoping you'd like this place as much as I do."

I eyed the house, then him, doubtfully. "No way in the world you moved that fast."

He laughed. "Nope. I've had this in the works for a while, but if you don't like it, I can sell it and buy a different one." He sounded like he was talking about changing a pair of shoes. I supposed when you had enough money, a house was no big deal.

"I've gone past this place a bunch of times," Cole said. "It looks amazing from the outside."

Toby held up a handful of keys and jiggled them back and forth. "Let's take a look on the inside, shall we?"

"Is this your grand gesture?" Cole asked him.

"It might be," Toby said.

"If it is, you planned to get in trouble in advance," Oliver pointed out. "Either you knew you'd fuck up or you like to have something up your sleeve." He seemed as though he wasn't sure if he should be impressed or not.

"Or I just needed somewhere to live," Toby suggested. He opened the door and stepped inside, leaving us to follow.

The entry foyer to the house was large, but not over-whelming. It could have felt cold, sterile and unwel-coming. Instead, it was cozy and warm. Both in temperature and in look. The floors were covered in mid-tone hardwood, which wasn't brand-new, but it wasn't tired either.

"There's an office through there, kitchen that way." Toby pointed. "This is what I wanted to show you first." He stopped in front of a pair of tall timber doors. He gripped the handles and slid them to either side, into the cavities in the wall.

Breath whooshed out of me.

"Holy shit."

Toby moved aside to let me walk a couple of steps and stand just inside the large room. Floor to ceiling were covered in bookcases. Leaning against one was a ladder on a rail that continued all the way around the room. Comfy chairs were scattered here or there beside low tables.

"This is incredible," I whispered, not wanting to shatter the moment. It was the perfect place to relax and read, and forget the rest of the world. The kind of room I'd dreamt of having since I was a kid.

Admittedly, my imagination pictured a secret door, but this was almost as good.

"It would be more incredible if there were books in here," Oliver said.

"Here's what I'm thinking," Toby said. "It'll take years to fill those shelves. That gives us something to work towards. And a good reason to buy all the books."

"Years?" I questioned. "I think you might be underestimating my ability to collect books." Give me one or two good book events and I could make some reasonable headway here.

"Luckily this place has lots of rooms," Toby said. "And enough land to extend the house. We could make a library as big as you want." He stretched his hands out wide.

"This is amazing, but I don't know that it's as simple as giving me somewhere to store books," I said.

He was trying, I'd give him that. And they were, after all, books.

"Lucky for me, I have something else to show you," Toby said.

"She's seen your cock," Oliver said.

"She's seen yours too, and judging by the body language, that wasn't enough for her to forgive you either," Toby told him.

"I'm still working on it," Oliver muttered.

"Yeah, well, come this way." Toby took my hand and led me out of the library.

"Don't tell me this place has its own rink," I said.

"You can tell me that," Cole said softly. "I've always wanted my own rink." Apparently whatever Toby's plans were, Cole was all in.

"Not yet," Toby said. "I might buy the house next door, tear it down and put in a rink. Let's put that in the 'maybe' basket."

I walked with him to the enormous kitchen. The cabinets were light timber, the island covered in white, veined marble. All of the appliances were big and obviously new. A chef could make a feast in here.

As for me, I could feel fancy while cooking ramen noodles or Vegemite on toast. I had many skills and interests, but cooking wasn't one of them. I preferred to eat. Although, I could make a mean margarita. Priorities.

From the island, Toby picked up a couple of sheets of paper. He handed them to me, an intense expression on his face.

I took them from him, adjusted my glasses and scanned the first page.

"You're—"

"Applying for Australian citizenship," Toby finished for me. "I wanted you to know I'm not going anywhere. This is my home now. Here, with you. All three of you. Like I said, if you don't like this place, we can find somewhere else. But you ain't getting rid of me that easy."

"That's wonderful," I said. I blinked away sudden tears.

In the back of my mind, I thought he might go back to America at some point and we'd never see him again. Part of my reluctance to forgive him was fear that as soon as I did, he'd be gone. That would break my heart all over again. And Cole's.

"Yeah, it is," Cole agreed. "I'm glad you're not going anywhere." He draped an arm over my shoulder and one over Toby's. He kissed me, then he kissed the other player. "I love you both."

"I love you too," I told him.

"Yeah, love you, bro," Toby told him. "Oliver, you're like the big brother I never had."

"Thank you for not saying I'm like a father to you," Oliver said, rolling his eyes toward the ceiling.

Toby chuckled. "Nah, one father is enough." He took the papers from my hand and placed them back on the island. "I have one more surprise for you. Wait here." He hurried out of the room, towards the front of the house.

Voices came from that direction, followed by the front door closing.

Toby stepped back into the kitchen, a food delivery bag in his hand. Giving me a meaningful look, he placed it down on the counter and opened it. He stuck in his hand and pulled out a hamburger wrapped in wax paper. He turned it around and opened it slowly. The burger on the palm of his hand, he held it up for all of us to see.

"Observe, a perfectly good hamburger with beetroot on it. I'm going to eat all of this, just for Marley. No matter how disgusting and potentially sacrilegious it is."

Oliver leaned his hip against the island and crossed his arms. "Don't let us stop you."

"Wait," I said. I pulled out my phone and opened the camera. "I feel like this is a good time to record the moment for a future giggle." I nodded at Toby to go ahead and eat.

He grimaced, but bit into the burger. His look of disgust was one of the funniest things I'd seen in a long time.

"How the fuck do you eat that?" he asked with his mouth still full. He chewed quickly and swallowed. "The shit we do for love." He took another bite and another, and went on eating until all of the burger was gone.

"Are you reconsidering applying for citizenship?" I asked. "I mean, if you're going to be one of us, you'll have to learn to eat those."

"Hell yes, and hell no," Toby said. "I'm never eating that again. By the way, I bought burgers for all of you too, if you're finished laughing at me."

I responded by playing back the video and giggling

at the look on his face. When it was finished, I started it again.

"Eating that shit was totally worth it to see you smile," Toby said. He pulled out the rest of the burgers and handed them around.

"That's good, because if Kage saw this, he'd be furious," I said. "You guys eating hamburgers during the season." I clicked my tongue and shook my head.

The fact Oliver hadn't lectured him already was another surprise. I had a suspicion he enjoyed watching Toby as much as I had. Cole too, although he was standing off to the side, looking bemused.

"Still worth it," Toby said. "Only… I'm out of grand gestures. Although, I could try to contact that author you love so much and see if I get an advance copy of her rugby romance book? I know some people."

"I wouldn't say no to that," I said. I glanced down at the burger in my hand.

I took a few moments to collect my thoughts and understand the way I was feeling. I didn't want to tell him what he wanted to hear unless I was completely sure of it myself. If I did that, the lie would be worse than the one they told me. I wasn't going to do that to them or to myself. I especially wasn't going to do that to my baby. They deserved the best start in life, including being surrounded by adults who cared enough to be honest with each other. Wasn't that what every kid needed?

I looked back up slowly. "I like the way this feels. Being here with you. I like this house. I love the library."

"I love *you*," Toby said.

I smiled softly at him and said, "I love you too. But if you ever do anything like what you did, ever again, I *will* send that footage to Kage and maybe the Internet as a whole."

The video would go viral in a matter of hours, if not minutes. He was famous enough that people would love seeing it.

"Ohhh, blackmail, I like it." Toby grinned. He pressed a hand to his chest, over his heart. "I solemnly swear I will never be a dickhead like that again. I've learned my lesson. I'm going to be a good guy from now on. I don't want to lose you." He wound his arms around me and kissed me gently.

"I don't want you to lose me either," I said. I kissed him back, lightly at first but quickly getting deeper.

Oliver's phone pinged with an incoming message. "Shit."

CHAPTER 30
MARLEY

"She's cute," Toby remarked.

"Very," I agreed.

We stood back near the door while Oliver held his newborn baby granddaughter. The expression on his face was nothing less than complete awe.

"She looks just like her mother," he said softly.

"Funny, all of my guys think they look like her," Cat said. She lay back in the hospital bed, looking exhausted but happy. When we arrived, she sent her boyfriends off to have something to eat, giving us time to spend with her.

Oliver scoffed. "She has your nose, eyes and chin. I can already tell she has a stubborn streak."

"Whose stubborn streak?" Cat teased. "I'm pretty sure that started with you."

"Yours, mine, whatever." Oliver smiled down at the

baby and kissed her forehead. "Either way, she's adorable. Just like you were."

Cole squeezed my hand. "It won't be long until we're holding our baby," he whispered.

"I can't wait," Toby also kept his voice down low. "I hope they look just like Marley. Although, they'd be doing well if they looked like me or Cole."

"I can hear you, you know," Oliver said, without looking in our direction. "The baby will be beautiful, no matter what. With Marley for a mother, how could they not?"

"You guys are sweet," I said."

"They're right," Cat said. "Your baby will be gorgeous. I can't wait for these two to play together."

"Have you decided on a name yet?" Oliver asked.

Cat smiled softly. "Her name is Sophie. Sophie Wendy Ryan, after Mum."

"She looks just like a Sophie," I said. Having the same last name as Cat was certainly easier than Sophie Brewer-Moss-Grant, or whatever order they chose to put the guy's last names. Baby Hammond was definitely easier than Baby Davies-Glover-Ryan.

"Yes, she does," Oliver agreed. "That's the perfect name. I was worried her fathers might insist on Puck or Winger."

Cat laughed. "Don't give them any ideas."

"Too late," Toby said with a grin.

"There's no way this baby is being named Puck Hammond," I said firmly.

"Of course not, that would be ridiculous," Toby said. "Puck is just a nickname. Right up until they forget what their actual name is."

"You really like eating hamburgers with beetroot on it don't you?" Oliver asked him.

Toby cleared his throat. "Good point. Puck is a terrible nickname. We're totally not going there. No way." He raised his hands in the air and swished them back and forth as if he could erase the last couple of minutes.

I shared a glance with Cole and we both laughed. He gave me a loving smile and a faint questioning raise of an eyebrow.

I looked back at Oliver. Seeing him with Sophie reminded me why I fell in love with him in the first place. He wasn't perfect, but he was one of the most loving, caring people I'd ever met. Going behind my back was a dick move, but all he wanted was to give me a moment like this. A perfect little life to bring into the world and love. It was the most fucked up, precious gift I'd ever been given.

I nodded once.

"Looks like the new mommy could use some rest," Toby said. He must have noticed the exchange between Cole and me. "Why don't we leave her to it?" He gestured meaningfully to Oliver.

Oliver kissed the baby again before placing her back in her mother's arms. He leaned down to kiss Cat's cheek. "I'll be back later to see how you're doing."

"Thanks, Dad." Cat smiled down at her daughter, pure love on her face. She'd never looked more beautiful or more happy.

I realised that, if I wasn't already pregnant, I would have wanted to be after seeing her like this. I guessed Oliver had a point. He knew me better than anyone. He knew what I needed before I did.

I took his hand as we stepped out of the room, into the corridor.

"I forgive you," I said. "Don't ever do it again, but I forgive you."

He pulled me to him and brushed his lips over mine. "I won't promise that I won't screw up again, but if I do it will only be to make you happy."

That was what I thought. He'd totally do it again. He was never going to stop thinking he knew best. That was something we were going to have to work on.

"Oliver—" I started.

He silenced me with a kiss. "I told you, you belong to me. That hasn't changed. It's my job to take care of you. I'm never going to stop doing that, whatever it takes."

"Hey, it's our job too," Toby said. "That and kicking ass out on the ice."

"Exactly," Cole agreed. "I'd say we all belong to each other."

"Sounds about right to me," I said. "Now, about that huge library…"

Each of the guys held a heavy bag of books in both hands. They carried them into the library and placed them down beside the door.

"You want us to put them on the shelves?" Toby offered. He leaned against the door frame and crossed his arms.

I looked around again at the extensive shelves and chewed my lip for a moment.

"I think I'll sort them out as I go," I said finally. "I don't know how I want to arrange them. I mean, do I go by genre, author or book colour?"

All three of them exchanged a glance. I could almost see them thinking, wondering if the last option was a joke or not. Should they laugh or was I serious? Would they offend me if they chuckled?

I watched all of this pass between them, my eyebrows raised slightly. Let them stew on that for a while. It wouldn't hurt them.

For the record, I preferred alphabetical, by author. Then by genre.

"At least she didn't suggest placing them with their spines facing the wall," Toby said.

"Do I look crazy?" I asked. I liked to be able to find my books without having to pull them out, one by one.

"You look beautiful," Oliver said. He grabbed my hand and pulled me to him.

"Is that so?" I asked. "I have to say I'm liking this

roguish look you have going on." I ran the tip of my finger down his stubbled cheek. "It's sexy."

"Really? I might let it grow out. I've always wondered how I'd look with a beard." He rubbed his chin with his thumb and forefinger.

"I might do that too, if that's what Marley goes for," Toby said. He rubbed his own chin as though he had a beard that covered half his chest.

"You don't need to have a beard to be attractive," I said. "If you want to grow one, that's up to you." I wasn't going to start telling them how to dress or what to look like. I trusted they'd give me the same consideration. Or else we'd be having words.

"I'll think about it," Toby said.

Oliver placed his hand on my cheek and turned my face to him before lowering his mouth to mine. "I missed you."

He kissed me like he'd never kissed me before in his life. As if he'd waited millennia for this moment. He kissed me with love, promise and desire.

I slid my arms around his neck and kissed him back, savouring the warmth of his lips and the taste of his mouth.

In the corner of my eye, I saw Cole step over to us. He stood behind me and lightly massaged my shoulders before moving his hands down to the hem of my shirt and back up underneath it.

Apparently not wanting to be left out, Toby moved

between Oliver and me and helped Cole to pull my shirt up and off over my head.

Cole unhooked my bra and he and Toby slid it off and dropped it to the floor. Toby cupped my breasts and started to massage my nipples.

At the same time, Cole knelt and pulled down my leggings and panties before helping me out of them.

While Oliver slipped his hand between my legs, Cole undid Toby's jeans and pushed them down his hips. He wrapped his fingers around the base of Toby's cock and his mouth around the head.

"I love a guy who knows what he wants," Toby said.

"I love you too," Cole said before swirling his tongue around Toby's tip and taking him back into his mouth.

"I know what I want," Oliver said. He worked loose the button of his own pants and pushed them down with one hand while pushing me to my knees with the other.

Kneeling side-by-side with Cole, I teased the head of Oliver's cock before taking him into my mouth as deep as I could. With him all the way down the back of my throat, I sucked, gagging when he thrust in deep.

"I'll never tire of your mouth," Oliver groaned.

"Funny, I was thinking the same thing," Toby said. In spite of that, he slid himself out of Cole's mouth and dug into his pocket for something before taking his jeans off the rest of the way. "Cole, clothes off. Now." In his hand, he held a small tube of lube.

Flopping onto his ass, Cole hurried to do what Toby

said. Stripping off his clothes and sending them flying every which way.

After a moment, Toby and Oliver did the same thing.

Toby gestured for Oliver to lie on the hardwood, on his back. Looking amused, Oliver actually did just that before pulling me to straddle him and slide down his cock.

Cole knelt right behind me and took the tube from Toby's hand to squirt some lube onto his fingers. He handed the tube back and smeared the cold lube onto my rear hole.

"Lean forward," Cole said. When I did, he pressed a finger into me, then another, readying me for his cock. He slid them in and out several times.

I moaned, enjoying the sensation of having two of my holes filled at the same time. It was like nothing I ever experienced before. I couldn't have described how good it felt if I wanted to.

"I want your cock," I whispered.

Oliver reached up to wrap his fingers around my throat. "Are you sure you're ready?"

"Very sure," I said, whimpering with anticipation.

Cole moaned and gripped my hips before pushing himself straight into my ass.

I cried out with the suddenness of his entry, but it turned into a moan of pleasure.

"Lean forward a bit more," Toby said.

I looked back over my shoulder to see Toby kneeling behind Cole, readying him for his own cock. Holy shit.

Cole swallowed audibly, but leaned forward, his head pressed against my shoulder. He groaned as Toby slid inside him.

We were all still for a while before Toby started to move. He set the pace, driving Cole deeper into me and pushing me onto Oliver.

It could have been a rushed, frenzied fuck, but we took our time, moving slowly and carefully in and out, on and off each other. The only sound in the library was panting, moaning and the rush of blood through my ears. I'd never felt so full or so complete. I never wanted this to end.

"I love you," I said to all three of them.

"We love you too," Cole said, his mouth near my ear.

"I'm going to come," I said. "Come with me. Please…"

I pitched over the edge, into the abyss, where the only thing that existed was pleasure and the sound of myself and my three guy's orgasms in unison, like a beautiful orchestra. The rest of the world ceased to exist for an eternity before time started to flow again like the juices of our arousal.

Panting and slick with sweat and cum, I flopped down onto Oliver, holding him close while Cole held me and Toby held all of us.

"I declare this library officially christened," Toby said.

I managed a breathless laugh. "Yes. Yes it is."

"Let's get cleaned up and christen the rest of the house," Oliver said.

"That's the best idea I've ever heard," Cole said.

"Is the first of many," Oliver said. "I have a lot more of them."

I picked up my head and gave him a stern look. He grinned, not even slightly apologetic.

"All of them are based on love," he said.

I hummed and slid off him. "I guess I'll find out if that's true or not."

"It's true, we have the rest of our lives for me to prove that to you." Oliver pulled me to my feet and, between my guys, we went to christen the first of the house's showers.

EPILOGUE

OLIVER

I tapped my phone against my thigh, waiting impatiently. The two figures who lay on the ground at my feet were getting restless. They struggled against the zip ties that held their wrists and ankles together. Both tried to shout past the duct tape across their mouths.

I thought about sedating them again, but that would be too easy. They needed to know what was happening. They needed to suffer.

Finally, a dark SUV rolled to a stop beside mine. The doors opened and two younger men stepped out.

"Hey, Doc," one of them greeted.

"Hunter." I gave him a nod. "Parker." They were identical, but I'd noticed Hunter tended to take the lead. Typical of the older twin.

"Hey," Parker replied. "Hunter said you had some assholes you wanted us to deal with?" He glanced down at the two figures rolling on the ground.

"I do. This is Jarrod and Zaden. They tried to rape my woman and her friend."

Hunter grimaced. "I hate rapists. Especially ones who try to touch our women. Don't worry, these two won't be touching anyone ever again. Ice Miller is going to have a shit load of fun with them."

"I'm sure he is," I said. "I know you'll be in touch when you need the favour returned."

"Count on it," Hunter said. "It's always handy to have a discreet doctor on the books."

The pair was as shifty as fuck, but we were useful to each other from time to time. Especially when it came to eradicating predators like these. The brothers would regret their own births by the time Ice was done with them. They'd certainly regret approaching Marley and Eden.

As for me, I had absolutely no regrets at all. They deserved everything that was coming to them.

I helped the twins to load the assholes into the back of the SUV.

"Thanks for the sugar pills," I said as Hunter closed the back of their vehicle. I didn't want to know where they got them from, so I didn't ask.

Hunter grinned. "They look legit don't they? You might be surprised to know how often they've come in useful."

"I can imagine," I said dryly. I stepped back towards my SUV and pulled my keys out of my pocket.

"Later, Doc." Parker waved before slipping back into the passenger seat and closing the door behind him.

"Yeah." I had a feeling it wouldn't be very long before I heard from the Brantley twins again. They were always up to something. I met them when I helped their brother Reuben and his girlfriend. One favour had led to another and the cycle continued. As long as people tried to fuck with our families, it would keep going. It was easier to have guys like this on my side than against me anyway.

I waited and watched as their tail lights disappeared into the night.

Satisfied, I climbed back into my car and drove home to my woman and her other two boyfriends.

Thank you for reading! Eden's story is in Pucking Hardened Hearts. The next release is Reuben Brantley's story, which starts in Possessive.

If you'd love a bonus scene with Marley and her men bringing new life into the world, you can read that here.

ABOUT THE AUTHOR

Maggie Alabaster writes reverse harem romance.

She lives in NSW, Australia with one spouse, two daughters, one dog, and countless birds.

Jo Bradley writes contemporary romance.

Sign up for Maggie's newsletter! Sign Up!

Join Maggie's reader group! Join here!

Follow Maggie on Bookbub! Click here to follow me!

Check out Maggie's website- www.maggiealabaster.com

Sign up for Jo's newsletter

ALSO BY MAGGIE ALABASTER

Sparrow and the Mafia Kings

Possessive

Ruined

Corrupted

Pucking Dark Hearts

Pucking Hearts Collide

Pucking Forbidden Hearts

Pucking Hardened Hearts

Dusk Bay Demons

Puck Drop

Breakaway

Power Play

Brutal Academy

Book 1 Heartless

Book 2 Cruel

Book 3 Vengeful

Court of Blood and Binding

Book 1 Song of Scent and Magic

Book 2 Crown of Mist and Heat

Book 3 Sword of Balm and Shadow

Book 4 Whisper of Frost and Flame

Dark Masque

Book 1 Bait

Book 2 Prey

Book 3 Trap

Saving Abbie

Book 1 Pitch

Book 2 Pound

Book 3 Session

Book 4 Muse

Book 5 Rhythm

Book 6 Encore

Novella Venomous

Saving Abbie books 1-4

Saving Abbie books 4-6 + Venomous

Ruthless Claws

Book 1 Ivory

Book 2 Crimson

Book 3 Elodie

Harmony's Magic

Book 1 Summoned by Fire

Book 2 Summoned by Fate

Book 3 Summoned by Desire

Shifter's Vault

Book 1 Discarded

Book 2 Deceived

Book 3 Disgraced

My Alien Mates

Book 1 Star Warriors

Book 2 Star Defenders

Book 3 Star Protectors

Academy of Modern Magic

Book 1 Digital Magic

Book 2 Virtual Magic

Book 3 Logical Magic

Complete Collection

Summer's Harem

Book 1: Shimmer

Book 2: Glimmer

Book 3: Flicker

Complete collection

Short reads

Taken by the Snowmen

Jingle All the Way

Also by Maggie Alabaster and Erin Yoshikawa

Caught by the Tide

Book 1–Pursued by Shadows

Book 2 Pursued by Darkness

Book 3 Pursued by Monsters